nF421029

Amy finds a man

a story by

Vincent A. Cronin, Jr.

Dedicated to
Jessica
who saves me
daily

1

"The next thing we do is find Amy a good man."

Amy took this in stride. "Oh, Charlie… I know you're riding high on our big win, but you don't get to solve what you think is a problem in my social life. Just enjoy the success." She took another sip of her wine.

Charlie was insistent. "Look, we three are brilliant. Our research, our investigation, and our argument just cost that evil miscreant five million and three years in prison. The senior partner who presented the case gave us the rest of the day off, and wants our help with his own case!" He took a breath. "And I don't love it that my beautiful and brilliant friend goes home to an empty apartment every night."

Dave looked at him and chuckled. "Sorry about that… it's just his third drink sentimental streak. I'll get him home."

"Oh, that's alright. It's a"Oh, that's alright. It's a ctually a sweet thought." Then Amy had a great idea. "Let's turn this into a feast. There's a place on the other side of the park where the sandwiches are huge, then we go home and pass out from eating too much."

The guys agreed, and lunch with lemonade was ordered. The conversation turned to the case they would face in the morning. They knew it was a hum-dinger.

After sandwiches, they cut through the park. Amy's apartment was five blocks away, and the guys were headed to their trains home. There were a few high fives and a little dancing.

"Hey, look." Dave had spotted something. He pointed toward a bench, with a man sprawled across it, leaning on a soft leather briefcase.

Amy was the first to arrive. "Sir? Are you alright?" She shook his shoulder.

"Careful, Aim... some of these guys get violent." Charlie was suspicious.

Amy continued. "Sir?" She moved his long hair off his face and almost screamed. "That's blood. He's bleeding, and unresponsive. I'm calling 911." It took the ambulance, park police and regular beat cops a few minutes to arrive, in which time Amy talked to the man, trying to reassure him that help was on its way.

The EMTs assured her that although he had some cuts and bruises, this man wasn't bleeding to death. He had apparently been attacked, possibly by more than one person, and his wallet was gone. The police were satisfied for the moment, and the EMTs said what hospital they were taking him to. Everyone took her contact information when she asked them to let her know how he was.

"Do you know this man, miss?" Plainclothes. A tall, well-dressed man in his thirties. Maybe a detective.

"No, never seen him before. I just don't think he's homeless or anything. I'm curious who he is."

"Well, good guess that he's not homeless, his clothes have been pressed recently. Maybe he can tell us something when he wakes up. Here's my card. Call me in a couple days."

Amy appreciated his manner. "Here's my card, detective DeVries. If you hear anything..."

"Thanks, and it's Paul. I'll let you know when I hear anything. Nice to meet you, Amy Leary, LLD. Thank you for stepping. Not everybody does that."

Amy blushed a little. "Glad I could help." She walked toward Charlie and Dave, who she knew would have a comment.

"Wow, Amy... got that poor defenseless detective in a spell... he's still watching you walk away." Charlie subtly (for Charlie) suggested.

"Hey, don't you two have trains to catch?"

Dave looked at his watch and they took off running. As she walked home, Amy wondered why she had gone out of her way for this complete stranger. Something had struck her about him when she saw his face. She couldn't figure out how, but she felt that he was important to somebody. The thought that she had gotten him some help made her smile.

Changing out of her work suit into home lounging gear, Amy found a piece of paper in the jacket pocket. She had forgotten in all the excitement that she had picked it up when it fluttered from the man's bag back in the park. It was a small piece of tan paper, folded in half. She looked, and saw a few lines of very neat printing.

> Days without you
>
> Are no longer days
>
> But years
>
>   of moonless, starless
>
>   dead blind night
>
> Punctuated only by the grind
>
>   and screech of the machinery
>
> And my resigned sighs.

She took a deep breath trying not to cry, but a tear was already formed. She let it roll down her cheek. Amy had to know who this mysterious stranger was, and what he was doing on that bench. She resolved to help this man any way she could. Starting right now. Amy dialed the number of the most literate person she had ever met.

"Hi, Deb... good... hey, I have a favor to ask. Do you still have that program that searches for quotes?... Cool, would you look something up for me?" Amy read the eight lines. There was a pause. "You've never heard it?... What does the program say?... Oh. Nothing in the last what? Two thousand years? It must be original, then... Okay, 99.999 percent...

"Oh, I was out celebrating with Dave and Charlie, and we found a man half laying on a bench. He was bleeding, so I called 911. A little piece of paper fell out of a bag he was clutching, and this was on it. Needless to say, I'm curious who he is, if he wrote it, or somebody wrote it to him... Right... Sure. Maybe you can get a handwriting match... that would be cool. I'll email it right now... got it? Yeah. Thanks hon, let me know."

Sleep wasn't going to be the easiest thing to do, with her mind coming up with multiple scenarios, but Amy was determined. Tomorrow at work might be a bear, if this senior partner lived up to his reputation for taking the toughest cases.

....

Two days later, Amy was fighting her way through some contracts when the phone rang. "Leary... Oh hi, detective... Paul... any word on our mystery man?... Oh, glad he's awake, though... sure, I could drop by... I expect to be out of here about six, and I'll grab a taxi... Great, I'll see you there." Amy spent the rest of the afternoon thinking of Paul's clear, smiling eyes, an unusual thing for her. After noting that she was getting carried away, it was back to the contracts for a while.

At the hospital, there he was again, his eyes smiling right at her. "Hi, Amy. He's right this way. They say he has amnesia. The only thing he remembers is a woman's voice telling him everything would be alright. I figure that if he hears that voice again, he might remember more. He's speaking well, articulate, just doesn't remember his name or anything." He led her to the room.

Amy saw the cleaned-up version of the man on the bench. "Hi. Told you it would be okay. You're looking much better."

The man looked at her and tears ran down his face. "You're real."

"Yup... Amy Leary, at your service." She went over to him and shook his hand.

"Sorry not to be able to introduce myself... can't remember... They've been calling me Joe."

"Aah, that's not half good enough. Let's see... something lyrical... light... and a little bit rare, I think. Mind if I call you Aidan?"

The man was stunned. "And sure your own kindness knows no bounds, to be callin' me after the Old Sod's ancient and gentle sun god." That had come out with a soft Irish accent. "Don't know where that came from... sorry if it's weird..."

One of the nurses was passing through. "Don't worry... he has flirted with the nurses in at least four different accents. Irish is new, though."

Amy had heard another clue. "And you know of Eodh, the old god. My mom used to tell me some of the stories. Any idea where you know him from?"

Aidan shook his head, seeming a little down. "But I like the name. Mind if I keep it?"

"As long as you want. Anything I can get you while I'm here?"

"Oh, just a few more minutes' company from someone who doesn't want to stick pins and tubes in me."

"You got it."

Forty-five minutes later, a doctor heard the loud laughter coming from the room and asked Amy not to get his patient so excited. "Let's talk in the hall. He really needs the rest. Two major head wounds, four cracked ribs, bruises all over, and a bruised knee. With all that, we can only keep him here three more days. Just to complicate things, we haven't found him anywhere to go next. The amnesia and no known medical coverage is making it hard."

Amy looked at Aidan, still chuckling from their conversation. She squinted, took a deep breath and spoke. "He can stay with me, if that's good enough."

Paul gasped. "You can't do that... perfect stranger! Could be a serial killer!"

Amy just smiled. "Ever since I was little, there's been this voice, my own voice, giving me guidance. Like, 'Don't step into the street' right before a car speeds by; or 'Don't eat at that restaurant' the day before they get condemned by the food police. I ignored it a twice. Once I slipped on some invisible ice and broke my hand, the second time I tried to tough out a cold and it turned into pneumonia. A week in the hospital. That voice is telling me to do anything I can for this man, and I'm going to." She stuck her hand into her jacket pocket, and felt the piece of paper.

"Oh... I forgot. This fell out of his bag when the EMTs came, and I picked it up. I'd like to give it back." Paul took it from her, and read it. Amy could see him fighting back a tear.

"Wow. Maybe he's a writer. A great writer." Paul handed it back.

Amy looked at the doctor. "Just another minute? Remembering it could help..."

The doctor nodded, and Amy went back in.

"Aah, my angel returns! But I see that something's up..."

"Yeah. I wanted to return this. It fell out of your bag, in the park."

Aidan read the lines. "Somebody with a soul's worth of loss. Vaguely familiar, like I read it twenty years ago, but I couldn't guarantee it's mine. Thanks." One more shake of Aidan's hand, and she was off.

Out in the hallway, Paul had some things to say. "I still think you're nuts, but in a nice way. I have some friends in National Security, and I'll see if they can help ID him. Meanwhile, be careful. And hope there's a room opening up somewhere."

The day came, and Amy took a cab to the hospital. Paul was waiting on the steps. "I brought a car, it's easier than calling another cab, and cheaper than having one wait."

Amy was suitably impressed by his thoughtfulness. "Thanks, that's sweet."

Paul added "Besides it gives me another chance to see you, and ask you out on a date. Dinner? Or lunch? Or coffee?"

Amy blushed. "Let me think about that." She walked through the front doors of the hospital smiling, and carrying a department store bag. When they arrived at Aidan's room, it was all made up, and he was nowhere in sight.

A nurse's voice from behind them intoned. "Thought I recognized you two. Nice couple. Aidan's down the hall watching TV. He was tired of the room."

Instead of protesting that they were not a couple, Amy looked at Paul and smiled uncomfortably, then headed down the hall. Aidan stood when he saw her. "You really don't have to do this, if you have the smallest reservations. I can find another way."

Amy shook her head. "There is no escape. You're going to be where I know you're safe, you're going to rest for what the doctor says could be a couple weeks, and you're going to recuperate. Besides, coming here to see you I've had more fun than I have for a long time. I could use a couple weeks of that. Here, I got you something." She handed Aidan the bag.

"What, a place to stay AND presents? I'm going to have to do something great in return." He opened the bag.

"For my convenience too. So you're not sleeping in jeans or wandering around naked in the middle of the night." She smiled.

Aidan was impressed. "Wow. Pajamas and a robe and slippers too. That's amazing. Thank you. Can we get out of here now? If I stay any longer they could find some excuse to keep me."

"I'm your transport. Got a car at the front door." Paul was still a little suspicious, but mostly convinced that Aidan could be a good guy. As they walked past the nurse's station, the voice from a few minutes ago called out.

"Oh no you don't. You don't get to walk. Hop into that wheelchair and an orderly will wheel you out. Hospital policy."

Aidan complied, mumbling "Orders. Always orders" under his breath. The response from behind the desk was "We all gonna miss you too. Come visit when you're yourself again."

As they got into the car, Paul asked "So what did they feed you in there?"

"Well, if you can call it feeding someone, salad, anemic burgers, cold lasagna, soup and tuna sandwiches. Even the cola was a bargain brand. Something tells me even a hospital could do better."

Paul chuckled. "You got lucky. A friend was in a hospital recently, all he got was jello and some nasty protein shakes. I had to smuggle in a pastrami on rye from the deli. You hungry by any chance?"

"Sure. Don't want to ask for more than I have already been given."

Amy was already on the phone. "Chinese for three alright?" Emphatic agreement ensued. "Hi, this is Amy Leary... Ni hao ma, Mister Ho... Yes, I'm very well today. And you? The family?... How's Lily doing in the new job?... Great. Could I get a Happy Family delivered to my place, please?... Yes, I'm almost there now... No, I'm not extra hungry, I have guests for dinner. Yes, I have guests... Thank you." She hung up. "Nosy old man... he's going to deliver himself so he can meet my imaginary guests. About twenty minutes." Then it struck her. "Oh, Paul... I didn't ask if you wanted dinner."

"Why yes, I'd be delighted. Have to leave by eleven, though. I've got Midnights this week."

When Mister Ho arrived, a little old man with four bags full to bursting with food that couldn't keep its scents in the bag, Paul jumped up and helped arrange things in the kitchen. Mister Ho looked at the men. He looked closely at a late invitation, Jack from across the hall. "You I know. Still owe five dollar."

Jack reached into a pocket and pulled out a ten. "Paid happily, with interest."

Mister Ho looked at Paul. "And you, Mister policeman. Good. You keep Amy safe." Then he shook Aidan's hand. "Amy hit you with book, give concussion?"

Amy took exception to that. "Now, Mister Ho... you know better. This is Aidan, or at least that's what I call him, who was mugged in the park. He's staying here while he recovers."

"Should recover own place."

Aidan smiled. "I'd be glad to. Can you tell me where that is?"

Amy chuckled. "He has amnesia, Mister Ho... doesn't know his real name."

Mister Ho nodded. "Scrambled brains, but not too much. You eat fish, unscramble. You be okay."

"And this nice detective is Paul DeVries. He's helping look for Aidan's identity."

Mister Ho went back to Paul. "You look hard. Will be in last place you look." He and Paul both smiled at the joke. "Okay, Miss Amy, you really have guests. Not imagination. Which one you dating?"

"Mister Ho! I'm not... These are friends; one old, two new. Just friends."

Mister Ho smiled. "Okay, friends. Enjoy Happy Family... I put dishes, teacups, good tea, and forks. Maybe someday everybody learns to use chopstick." He was still mumbling to himself as he left, and with a wave he was gone. Amy closed the door with a big smile. It was charming that this 90-year-old Chinese man considered her his granddaughter.

"Dig in, folks... we've got a lot of food here!"

Halfway through his first plateful of lobster and vegetable fried rice, Jack had a thought. "Hey, Aidan! What happens if you need something during the day?"

"Dunno. Hadn't thought about it.1 Don't know."

Jack grinned his Cheshire Cat grin. "I do. You come across the hall and knock. I work at home, and I have a project that will keep me in all day every day. Anything you need. In fact..." he reached into his pocket "...here's Amy's extra key. In case you want to do laundry, or walk the halls." He looked over at Amy, who smiled and nodded.

"Thanks, Jack. I probably won't be moving around too much this first couple days."

The conversation turned to the news, the weather and a couple movies people had seen recently. Aidan fell asleep. As Amy ushered Jack and Paul out, she whispered to Paul "Thank you. This can be counted as the best first date ever. Call me." She reached up and kissed his cheek. "Good night." And the door closed.

Fortunately, Amy had fallen for one of those promotional 60-piece sets of storage containers. She used eighteen to store the leftovers. Then, she brought out sheets and a pillow. Aidan was dozing. "Hey... wake up a little. Time for pajamas and some real sleep." Fortunately again, she had invested in a queen-size foldout. Aidan opened his eyes and saw the pajamas dangling before him.

"Oh, sorry... didn't mean to..."

"You have perfect timing. I had to kick them out anyway, so I could sleep. Work in the morning, you know, being Monday and all. Have to be alert."

He took the nightclothes and headed for the bathroom. "There's a red toothbrush there, new in the case just waiting for you."

When he came out, he was feeling humbled. "Thank you again. Really, I'll find a way to repay all this some day." He melted onto the couch and was asleep in seconds.

"No worries, sweet dreams."

In the morning Amy left at 7:30, setting a $20 in a bowl on the table. Aidan was left alone with a lot of Chinese food and a craving for egg, sausage and cheese in an English Muffin and an apple fritter. And coffee. He hoped that Jack was awake. Knock knock.

Jack was indeed awake. "Hey, neighbor... is there someplace to go for coffee?" Jack responded in the positive, pointing him to the semi-industrial looking machine on the kitchen counter. Aidan gleefully poured himself one.

"Whatcha up to?" Seemed like a simple question.

Jack had a not-so-simple answer. "Trying to come up with some unique images for ads, not having much success. Maybe I don't know enough about theatre in the park."

"What, Shakespeare?"

"No, this group is going to do new plays. Some one-acts, some full length. They sent copies of the plays for me to read, but I'm not getting ideas."

Aidan tugged at his chin as if he had a beard. "Any idea what 'Shakespeare in the Park' posters are going to look like this year?"

Jack rummaged around and found a brochure, handed it over. All but one of the images were photographs. Aidan took a gulp of coffee and stared at some sketches Jack had started. He squinted. "Hey, do you know that artist, did a bunch of stuff Art Deco? Mooka? Is that a name?"

Jack was stumped. "Moo... Muo... Mucha! Alphonse Mucha?"

"Think of a few precise, flowing black lines, beautiful woman..."

Jack lit up. "That's it! Alphonse Mucha!"

"Yeah, that sounds right. Maybe a good way to get contrast with the other guys' photos, graphically speaking, is something like that."

Jack was excited. He held up a book. "Like this!"

Aidan smiled. "Yeah maybe just one splash of color somewhere."

Jack had become enthusiastic. "Yeah, right. That I can do. Jeez, Aidan... for a guy that doesn't know his own name, you sure know some other stuff. You have just saved me. I have to turn in the proposal Wednesday, now I know what I'm doing. Can I get you anything besides coffee?"

Aidan confessed his craving from earlier. Jack checked his wallet, did a little happy dance, and flew out the door. "Stay right there. Five minutes tops."

After a very satisfying breakfast sandwich and a huge fritter, Aidan returned to Amy's. The question became what to do with the rest of the day. After half an hour of reading and about the same amount of daytime TV, he gave up. Straightening up the little pile of magazines, he noticed the dust. Not much, so he'd be able to take care of it. With a little searching, he found a vacuum but nothing resembling a duster. Time to bug Jack again.

Cleaning took all morning. As soon as one thing got cleaned, something else looked dirtier than it had before. Aidan kept after it, and at noon he lay down on the couch. An hour and a half later when his eyes opened, he wondered if this was why the doctor had recommended rest. He took Jack's cleaning supplies back shaking his head. Doctors don't know everything.

"Aidan! My muse! Come in, and see what you've inspired!" Jack had completed two posters. The flowing lines and bright blue in the woman's eyes made one stand out, and the other, with a hand with sparkling red fingernails holding a martini glass could grab a person's attention from some distance.

"Damn you're great. This is exactly it. Sure would get me curious."

"That's the job... get people to look, then tell them what's happening, where and when. Two more and I've got enough for the proposal. If I get the job it's twelve posters, at two thousand apiece, or ten percent of the ticket sales. I haven't decided. Hey, what are you doing for lunch?"

"Hadn't thought about it. Maybe Chinese."

"Bah Humbug. There's a great deli ten minutes away. I'll pick up a couple sandwiches. What do you like, pastrami, corned beef, maybe tongue or maybe a nice chicken salad?"

"Gosh all that sounds good. Corned beef and Swiss on a dark rye, a little dot of mustard comes to mind. Don't know from where."

"You got it, pal." Aidan held out the twenty, but Jack waved him off. "You just made it possible for me to work. I don't know if I'll ever let you pay. This time of day, it could take forty minutes to get two sandwiches. Have some more coffee, relax... I shall return."

When Amy got home at 6:35, Aidan was asleep sitting up on the couch. The sheets, pajama and robe from last night were neatly folded on a chair. And something seemed different. There was a smell in the air. She noticed the vacuum tracks in the carpet, and knew what it was. She sat on the couch next to him and nudged.

"You cleaned."

Waking up, he mumbled "Wha?"

"You cleaned. You didn't have to do that. I mean thank you, but the doctor said to rest, not to work. I see the twenty is still there. Did you eat?"

"Yup. Jack went out and got us breakfast and lunch."

"That's unusually generous of him..."

"He needed a direction to go with his project, I found him one. He got very excited about the whole thing."

"Cool. Want some General Tso's chicken?"

"I could do that."

Aidan hurried to finish a mouthful and wipe his mouth before asking "Do you ever cook?"

Amy chuckled. "I tried a couple times. First time I made charcoal-coated chicken, second time I made toxic stew. Gave up on behalf of anyone I might feed. You?"

"Not totally sure, but maybe. Ordering out feels like something special. Especially a feast like this."

Jack came over a little later. "Mister Magic here took one look at some work I was doing, hit the nail on the head. Said try it like Alphonse Mucha, and all of a sudden everything worked. The theatre people are going to love it, the people giving them the advertising grant are going to love it, and eventually I'll be famous."

Amy looked at him like he was a bit overexcited. "So who's Alphonse Mucha?"

Both men looked at her like she had skipped grade school. Jack responded. "Famous artist. You've heard of Art Deco?"

"Sure. Really nice jewelry."

"And some fantastic, ground-breaking art. Mucha was part of that. Hey! We've learned something about Aidan! He knows about art... at least some things."

Aidan made an approving face. "Impressive. Wonder if it can help narrow down who I am." There was a general agreement that if they found enough details like that, his identity would reveal itself. Aidan took the blank notebook out of his bag and wrote "Art."

Amy was curious about this artist. Jack brought over his book and the three talked about art. She was surprised at the history, sociology and even psychology that made it into the discussion.

The next morning, Amy looked Aidan straight in the eyes and said "Rest. Just rest."

He grinned. "Okay. At least I'll try."

As soon as she left, he dumped everything out of his bag. When he reached in for the notebook last night, he thought he had felt something odd. With the contents out, he reached in to the bottom, found a seam and pulled. Some Velcro gave way, and spilled the contents of what was apparently a secret compartment: ten stacks of hundred dollar bills, ten bills in a stack. Aidan wondered why.

Why was he carrying so much cash? Was he a criminal? Was he a rich guy who likes to buy things for cash? No scenario he came up with rang a bell. Maybe he could find out if the money had been involved in any crimes. It all looked brand new, the kind of bills you get at the bank. He even thought, and this seemed as likely as anything else, that he might be carrying around gifts for his ten kids. The thought made him chuckle.

It took Aidan almost a half hour to come up with a plan. He would call Paul.

An hour later, Paul showed up. "What's going on?"

"Hi, Paul... come in. I found something, and I wonder if you could find out about it." He revealed the cash.

"Wow. And you say this doesn't ring any bells..."

"Right. I wondered if you had a way to find out if it's connected to a crime."

Paul thought for a moment. "Well, if I look the serial numbers up on the Treasury website, and they have a criminal history, they go into evidence." He scratched his head.

"But then again, I know a guy. He can find out exactly when they were printed. I figure that if they're a week old, for instance, they have very little chance of problems. Beyond that, it becomes a lost-and-found kind of thing. The bills would be held as evidence until somebody claims them."

"Let's try your guy." Aidan was already forming plans for what to do with at least some of the money. Paul made the call, and read three serial numbers into the phone.

The results came back in seconds, and Paul started smiling. "Dude! They were printed four days ago. There's no doubt that these bills have gone from the Mint to a bank and into your hands. Nothing to worry about."

Aidan was a little relieved, but sad. "I almost wish they had a history. Might have provided a hint about who I am."

"Well, I can't say much about what your real name is, but as far as I can tell you're probably one of the good guys. One of the best. Literate, social, good sense of humor... not much more than that to ask for, really."

"Look who's talking. That means a lot. Thanks. Oh... if I get on it, I can do something nice for Amy! Would it be rude of me not to offer you a drink?"

Paul sensed what Aidan was trying not to ask him to leave. "I'll be in touch. We have a couple patrol officers flashing your picture around the park. If you're a regular, they might get lucky."

"Thanks. See you again soon."

As he pondered the things he could do with the money, the thought of' 'something for Amy' flowered in his mind. But what could he do? Hmmm... cook dinner? He could cook? Dishes started showing up in his imagination. Roasts of beef, chicken, fish, things to do with vegetables, and even desserts. He understood how to make each one.

He grabbed two piles of the cash, and put the rest back in its Velcro hiding place. Across the hall, he knocked gently. It was 10:30, but artists tend to sleep late. Fortunately, Jack was up and alert. "Dude! Come for breakfast?"

"Nope. Need some help with a project."

"Cool. What can I do?"

"I want to outfit Amy's kitchen, and make dinner."

"Awww, man... she'd freak but I can't afford to..."

Aidan grinned. "No need. I have cash. Found it hidden among my stuff. What I don't have is a charge card to get things delivered. I'm hoping you do."

Jack pulled him inside. "I trust the neighbors, but only so much. How much are we talkin'?"

Aidan pulled the cash out of his pocket. "Two thousand. Paul just confirmed that it's probably not stolen, and it is real. Hoping you could charge a few things and take the cash. How about it?"

"Hell yeah. Let's freak out my best neighbor." After an hour of shopping at a department store and a grocery, Aidan was done. "Congratulations, neighbor... you just dropped twenty two hundred, once you count the tip for delivery! And OMG, the stuff! You pick like you know exactly what you're doing."

"Yeah. Seems like I do. Right after Paul left, I started thinking what I could do with the money, and I just thought 'Something nice for Amy... maybe cook dinner". Then all these recipes came flooding into my head. Everything from Mac-n-cheese to Boeuf Bourgignon. I knew how to do them all."

"So... you're a chef?"

Aidan wasn't sure. "I have the vague impression that I love good food, so I learned how to make it."

"That means you found the time and energy to learn how. And that means that whatever you do for a living leaves you with free time, and apparently pays quite well. Dude, you might be rich. Sorry your plan fell through for tonight, but everything will be here at 10:00 in the morning."

"Yeah. You know if there's a Greek restaurant that can deliver?"

Jack was stunned for a moment. "Oh! I do know a Greek place. Spectacular stuff, a little pricey, but amazing. It's about a mile away."

"Okay. Can we call them and have dinner for three delivered at say 7:00 tonight?"

Jack looked the number up and started dialing. "Hi, can I have dinner for three delivered at 7:00 tonight? Yeah? Oh... I have the menu right in front of me... " After some discussion, a few 'what's that's' and a little more strain on Jack's credit card, he hung up. "There goes another hundred and fifty, I'm sorry to say. They guarantee enough food to feed four."

"Sweet. I'll just run over and grab a couple more bills, so you're not in the hole for my extravagant lifestyle."

"Hey, speaking of which, any other memories come to you?"

"Sure. A couple of libraries, art museums, and this one man's voice telling me I can do something better."

"Cool. Sounds like any day now you'll know everything."

"Yeah. Then I can invite you, Amy and Paul to my place, if I have one. I'll just go get those bills. Oh, do you have Amy's phone number?"

"Sure."

"Might be a good idea to tell her not to pick up dinner."

"Yeah. Will do."

2

When Amy arrived home, mystified at the idea that she shouldn't pick up dinner, there was just enough time for explanation before the food was delivered. Seeing what you get as dinner for three, Amy and Jack proceeded to invite three of their neighbors to dinner. After an hour and a half of festive cheer, all the food had actually been finished. The neighbors went home, and Jack made an excuse of having to finish his fourth poster.

Once the trash was taken out, Amy plopped onto the sofa, seeming preoccupied. Aidan sought to help. "Hey, got troubles?"

She shook her head. "Oh, not really. It's just this case I'm working on. Missing money, missing people, office politics, maybe some industrial espionage. I can't seem to get a complete image of what happened. Our client is likely to be charged with stealing the money, but he swears he didn't do it. It's a family owned business, and two family members are missing. On top of that, the plans for some proprietary technology they were developing have disappeared. Wiped from computers. I can't figure out where to start."

"Wow. Sounds like a mess. Like most extended families. Hope this nutrition helps."

Amy smiled. "In case I hadn't said it already, thank you for dinner. I don't eat like that most of the time, heck I would weigh a ton. But this was nice. And it's rare that I can have the neighbors over." She leaned back and closed her eyes.

Aidan had a thought. "How about this: instead of trying to imagine this whole big picture, investigate each thing as an isolated item. Often enough, if things are connected the connections show up along the way."

"Wow. Yeah. The only thing that's critical right now is the missing money. We don't have to explain anything else."

"And money isn't the hardest thing to track. Be sure to get the images."

"Images?"

"Of the checks, if there are any. There are two ways money can go missing: crooked accounting, which a forensic accountant will find, or forgery. Changing the amount on a check isn't all that difficult, but if the amount changes, you can get an idea where it changed. All banks, the Federal Reserve, and most big companies will have images of every check they handle."

Amy looked at him with awe. "So how do you know all this, Mister Mystery?"

Aidan was surprised too, but found it amusing. "No idea. Maybe I'm a crook." They both laughed at the thought.

Wednesday morning seemed to Aidan a good time to try to remember something. If not his own name, then something. Anything before waking up in the hospital. Meditation didn't seem to get him anywhere, so he started doodling in his notebook. He had already filled two pages with images, ideas, and phrases that had occurred him, so he started a fresh page. Some while later, a drawing emerged. Quite a respectable sketch of a cabin in the woods. It seemed to him that if he didn't already own such a thing, he should work to attain one. The sketch brought a tear to his eye. Only one, but a guy notices such things. This sketch was important.

The guys from Macy's rang the doorbell at exactly 10:00. "Delivery for Aidan Bench…"

He buzzed them in. "Hey, guys… put everything in the kitchen."

Five boxes later, they were done. "Pots, dishes, glasses, flatware and assorted kitchen implements. Order delivered. I'm supposed to confirm with your Jack Donlon. Unusual, but hey that's what it says on the order."

Aidan crossed the hall and knocked. "The kitchen stuff is here. Why do they have to confirm with you?"

"Partly because it's my credit card, and partly because I want to see all this stuff in person. Besides, I have I.D."

"Show-off. Come on and sign for it."

The folks from the grocery store arrived an hour later, covering every surface in the apartment. Unpacking that first, the two men realized the enormity of stocking the kitchen. They had filled the fridge, the canned goods shelves, and had herbs sitting on the counter.

Once they got the Macy's boxes emptied, Jack realized that there was a job ahead. "Dude. That's a whole lot of dishwasher time. If you're just using Amy's dishwasher, it'll take all night."

"Yeah." Aidan stretched, and put his hands behind his head, trying to think of how to shorten that time.

Jack beat him to it. "Ooh! We could ask the neighbors! Now that we have fed them, if you use yours, mine, and maybe three more…"

"Oh god that would be brilliant."

"I'll knock on some doors. You divide it all up into dishwasher loads. Everybody has the same model, so gauge by the one here." Jack ran out before Aidan could even thank him. When Jack came back with good news, Aidan remembered. "Don't you have a presentation to do?"

Jack grinned his Jack grin. "Postponed. I sent them pictures of the posters I did, and I'm now meeting with the whole theatre company, the money people, and the grant people from the state. They said that most of the time that takes three meetings across a couple weeks. My contact says I have 90% won this thing already. Most original art they've seen."

When Amy opened her door at 6:30, she first did a double take thinking she had gotten to the wrong apartment. She looked again, and recognizing her sofa, screamed. "AIDAN!!! What have you done?"

Jack came running down the hall. Amy turned to him. "And you! You're in on this too, aren't you?" He just nodded.

The table was set for dinner, and there were candles. Aidan came calmly out of the kitchen. "Hi there. Thought I'd make dinner. Had to get some supplies. Want a glass of wine first? We have a very nice Chardonay."

Amy considered, wondering what kind of madman she had let into her apartment. She had thought that he would sleep most of the time. "Sure. Some wine sounds like a fine idea."

Aidan poured her one. "And don't worry... if you really don't like or want the stuff I got, I'll take it with me once I remember who I am."

A couple sips in, Amy found her calmer voice. "So what smells so good?"

Aidan grinned. "Turkey meatloaf, roasted little red potatoes, and Brussels Sprouts. With apple tarts for dessert."

"So you can cook!"

"Apparently. And I can show you how while I'm here."

"Up for a challenge, are ya?"

Aidan grinned again. He really liked his new friend, and was grateful for everything she had done. "You'll pick it up in a snap. Couldja eat?"

"I could. Come on, Jack, let's see how good Mister Mystery really is."

Once they had each polished off an apple tartlet, the general concensus was that dinner was a raging success. "Well, we know one more thing about you. You've done this before. Any chance you own a restaurant?"

Aidan was feeling modest. "Doesn't feel like it. More like I like to cook."

"So anyway, between the wine and the tryptophan, it's going to take coffee for me to walk into the bedroom." Amy seemed very content.

"We got that, too. Jamaican. Want one, Jack?" Jack nodded.

....

Thursday turned out quiet. No big plans were made, nothing much to do. Aidan was noting images and some conversations he thought he remembered in his notebook when Jack showed up. "Hey Jack... maybe you can give me an opinion on something."

"Sure. Anything."

"I was doodling, and this image sort of appeared. Without me trying." He opened the notebook to the page with the sketch on it, and handed it over.

Jack's jaw dropped. "How long did this take?"

"Maybe 20 minutes, something like that."

"Well holy moly, Batman. One, this is gorgeous. Two, it's a place you know well, and care about. Three, this is a sketching style that not everybody uses." He looked closer. "What kind of pen is this?"

Aidan reached into his bag and showed the pen. "It was stuck in the wire binding."

Jack unscrewed the barrel, and examined the refill. "Yup. You, my friend are an artist. You've got a thirty dollar technical refill in a five dollar pen. Only really picky people do stuff like that. Hey... I have a thought. Mind if I take a picture and ask around if anybody recognizes the hand that drew this? Each artist has unique things they do. Maybe we can find your name."

Aidan wasn't convinced. But acceded. "Okay, go for it. You really think it's that good?"

"Yeah. I know some people in the art scene who would take it on like a trivia question. I'll take the picture, attach it to an e-mail..." Jack manipulated his phone as he talked. "And send it to all my art contacts, asking 'Do you know this artist?' and they'll get back to me. Piece of cake."

The two men sat back with some coffee and watched a detective show on TV. Aidan considered that this quiet day might turn out good after all.

Amy got home early, smiling from ear to ear. "You are a good luck genius. As soon as we started looking at the images of the checks, we figured out where the culprit was, and a quick conversation with a department supervisor yielded a lead. I called Paul, and he was free to go over to the company so he did. As soon as this forger knew the jig was up, she confessed. Been doing it for almost thirty years, a little at a time."

Aidan was impressed. "So was it your client's company?"

"Nope. One of their suppliers. They had always insisted on paper checks because the owner was kind of anti-tech, suspicious you know. After this, if they stay in business, they're going all digital. Our customer is off the hook."

"Way cool."

"Oh... and there's something else. My mom is coming in to town tomorrow to go to the theatre with some friends. She's liable to stop in for dinner. You don't have to stick around, Jack would probably like some company for a while."

Aidan wondered. "If it's not too weird explaining what I'm doing here, I would actually love to meet your mom. Tell her what a terrific job she's done, what a fine and wonderful daughter she has."

"Oh god, you even flatter me the way she does. You two will get along just fine. Okay. Be warned, she might get here a little before six. She usually brings food."

"I'll make space."

Amy had one more thing. "I'm going out tonight. For dinner."

Aidan had to ask. "Paul?"

"Yes, Mister Nosybody, Paul. Just dinner, so I'll be back in a couple hours."

"No rush. Enjoy yourself." Amy came in quietly at 10:30. Aidan pretended to be asleep, and smiled to himself.

Friday morning, Amy swept out of the bedroom smiling broadly. "Well, despite the fact that you're dying of curiosity I'm going to tell you about my date. Paul is the perfect gentleman, who lives in a brownstone with his brother. The place has been in his family for a hundred years, and there's a trust that pays the taxes, utilities and upkeep.

"He cooked for us, we had dinner, and sat around talking. He has the biggest collection of those 'For Dummies' books I've ever seen. Apparently, he read a book as a teen that advised among other things, 'know the ways of all men'. So when he meets someone who does something he doesn't know about, he buys and reads the corresponding book. The latest one is "Lawyers for Dummies" so he can know some of what I'm talking about.

"The man's a sweetheart. He wants us to move, at some acceptable pace to me, toward getting married. He sounded pretty sure about it."

"So, not fly-by-night."

"Definitely. Hope I wasn't seduced by the gorgeous house and great food. Nah, The look in his eyes and the nature of the kiss goodnight tell me I could spend a lot of time with him. I just like the guy."

"So enjoy that. And congratulations. Now off to work. It's going to take me hours to be presentable for your mother."

Aidan guessed that he was in the calm before some storm. Maybe his identity, maybe lots of things. The right thing to do was conserve energy, so as soon as Amy left for work, he went back to sleep. Being awake had become a fight not to take too many pain killers. Everything ached. At the hospital, they had said this would happen, and assured him that as long as there was no sharp pain, his body was doing the best it could to heal. He took them at their word.

Back up at 11:00, Aidan guessed that it would be a good time for lunch. The last of the Chinese chicken, and a Greek spinach dish went well together. Then it was stretches and muscle time. Pushing against the door frame would never replace weights, but it did use some strength.

Jack came by at 1:30, ebullient. "Best meeting EVER! I set the stuff up, explained how I would adapt the images to different spaces, like subway cars, and it took all of five minutes for thirty-five people to say yes. I not only got this assignment, but a request from a theatre to submit proposals for the rest of their season. I've made it to the big leagues!"

Aidan stood and hugged him with one arm. "Congrats! Wish we had some wine left."

Jack looked worried, noticing Aidan leaning on the cane. "Leg going bad?"

"Aah, just lack of movement, probably. I'll swing it around later and be good as new."

"If you say so. And hey… wouldn't have happened without you. I haven't forgotten. Oh, and nobody got back to me yet, on the sketch but they will. No wine for me… I got enough work for a month. See you around."

He wasn't through the door when his phone buzzed. "Hi... yeah?...where? and when?... oh, thanks. Let me know." He turned to Aidan. "This friend of mine showed the sketch to a gallery owner, who swears he has seen it somewhere. That exact sketch. They'll let me know."

Sitting down again felt good. Laying down felt better. The thought that his real name might be on the way was both a relief and a source of tension. Did he really want to know, and disturb the great time he was having with Amy and Jack? Not sure. The thought sent Aidan back toward sleep.

A little after 4:00, 4:11 to be exact, there was a key in the door. "Amy, hon... I'm here... brought food...did you..."

Aidan thought the voice somewhat familiar. "She's not here. Hope I can help."

The woman at the door stopped halfway through, and stared at him. Her eyes went wide, her jaw slacked. "Will..." Her eyes closed and the two bags in her hands dropped to the floor. Aidan got to her before she had a chance to melt to the floor.

"Lane!" As he crossed to her, his knee protested, and he managed to fall under her, arms around her. He counted that as a success. "Lane... come on, wake up... no fainting... let's get over to the sofa..."

The woman opened her eyes. "Will... what are you... where have you been?" She punched his arm, hard. He flinched from the pain. There were still bruises.

"What's that for?"

As she stood and picked up her bags, "You disappeared. Right after graduation, nobody could find you, you bastard!"

"Oh, that." He stood up and limped over to the sofa. "I didn't really graduate. They let me cross the stage with everybody, and handed me a blank piece of paper."

Lane stopped working in the kitchen. "What? You were the smartest person in that whole school. You had things to teach the teachers!"

"Doesn't matter if you don't turn in the assignments. I was six credits short. After graduation I was so embarrassed I literally ran away. Went to New Mexico, or more accurately ran out of bus fare there."

Lane was staring at him. "I do want to hear the rest of this, but I've got a surprise for you. My daughter is 26 years old, and I haven't seen you in almost 27 years. You do the math." She grinned.

A little calculation on the fingers. Then the light bulb flashed to life. "She's..."

"That's right, bud... she's your daughter. If you hadn't disappeared, I would have told you."

"She talks about her dad."

"Right. Remember Andy Brell?"

"Sure. Nice guy."

"He asked me out about a week after graduation. He had gotten his first job, and accepted to grad school. We went out to celebrate. A month later, I figured out I was pregnant. When I told him, he proposed on the spot. "He's still a good guy. He took Amy on as his own, and we have a 20-year old son, Patrick. Andy happens to be in China for the next six months, doing research and consulting in Urban Planning. So why exactly are you here in this particular apartment?"

William MacLeish, as he suddenly knew his full name, took a long pause. "Sorry. Things flooding back into brain." He paused again. "Almost two weeks ago, I was mugged and beaten. Amy found me unconscious on a park bench, and called 911. After a few days, the hospital couldn't keep me and there wasn't a bed available elsewhere. Amy had been visiting in the hospital and we had a great time, so she offered me her couch. I've been here since Monday, recuperating."

Lane shook her head. "The lost and in need. When she was little, she carried a handful of bandages and some antibiotic cream in case any of her friends hurt themselves. Tried to adopt a dozen dogs and cats. If someone was sad, she was always there with a hug. That's who your daughter is. But how about all those other years?"

"Oh, that. A couple years after I left, I met a guy in a bar, who said he'd love to be a literary agent. I told him I had written a few nice short stories in school and he could be my agent. We had a few drinks, and agreed to split any money if they got published. We spent a couple months re-creating them, polishing them. He turned the stories into a book and it was picked up almost immediately. We called the book 'Thessalon' for no particular reason. That darn thing is still selling 25 years later."

Lane looked shocked. "Thessalon? You are Ari Cantor?"

Will chuckled. "One of three pseudonyms."

Lane went over to the shelf. "She won't go anywhere without it. Read it when she was nine, keeps re-reading it." She handed him a copy of his first book with appropriately yellowed pages, ready to fall apart. Tears appeared in Will's eyes.

"So anyway, for the last twenty-five years I have published two or three books a year. Oh god, Seamus. I need to make a call." He kissed Lane. "Thank you. Seeing you brought me back." He rushed to the phone.

"Hey, Seamus... yeah... I got mugged on my way to the store... no, I'm okay now... no, they didn't get it... I had amnesia... memory just came back a few minutes... right... hey, that's a great idea. So one of us has constant control... something could happen to you, too... right... make it for either of us if something happens to one, the other has control... right... see you then... right... 526 E 83rd, #7... I'll be here."

"He says he'll have a lawyer here in an hour, which in his perspective on time means anywhere up to two. Says if I'm going to run around getting attacked, we need a contract that gives him full control over the work. Makes sense, so there's no doubt."

Lane was mumbling to herself, shaking her head. "Why pseudonyms? What do the other two pseudonyms do? Where do you live? Are you married?"

Will wasn't used to so many questions. "We'll need coffee."

"Oh, Amy doesn't have a coffeepot."

"She does now, and a bunch of other stuff. Poor girl was living on takeout. I said I would teach her to cook."

"And you cook."

"True. To start answering your questions, I'm not married, I spend most of my time at my cabin in the woods... Oh! The cabin! Harvey! He'll be going nuts. We haven't been apart more than three days before! I have to make another call."

When Will came back from the phone, Lane asked, rather delicately "Harvey?"

Will chuckled. "My dog. When he was a puppy, he looked kind of like a rabbit, so fluffy. A friend is going to bring him down in a couple days."

"So back to your story. Your pseudonyms."

"The other two names I write under write Romance and Mystery. L. S. DuPont and Yuri Ivanov, respectively. The pseudonyms help me write differently under each name. Hey, Amy will be here presently. Are we going to tell her?"

Lane blinked. "I've never held anything back from her, except her conception. She'll be overjoyed that you got your memory back, let's lead with that. Then the fact that we knew one another in school, then the bombshell."

"Okay. Here's your coffee. So it's your turn. What have you been doing for all this time?"

"My story is not so eventful as yours. I've been teaching. Eighth grade Language Arts. Trying to convince 12 and 13 year olds that they can use English well and that the effort is worth it."

Will was grinning broadly. "Would a visit from an author help?"

The phone rang, and Lane answered. "Hi, honey... Yeah? Who's Paul?... yes, I've met your guest, he's charming... oh, okay... see you then." She turned to Will "Who is Paul?"

"Police detective, showed up when Amy called 911 on me. Good guy. When I woke up in the hospital, he was there. He's been looking for my identity since. Why?"

"Amy's going to be late. She's stopping for drinks with Paul."

"Oh good. The way those two look at one another... I knew they could be more than friends. Cool. Oh gosh, that's another phone call"

Reading Paul's number from his card, Will dialed. "Hey Paul... Something just jogged my memory... yeah, they said this could happen... William MacLeish, author... I live out in the country upstate... right, came into town on a shopping trip... no, I had nothing obvious on me, just the hidden compartment in my bag... yeah... don't tell Amy, would you? I'll tell her when she gets home... thanks, dude...dinner on me somewhere outrageous some time... see ya"

Once Amy recuperated from the shock of all the news waiting for her at home, she hugged her mother, and hugged Will. "Actually, that explains a lot. The wise, wry smile on Dad's face when he looks at me, right up to why I trusted you enough to have you stay here. It's going to take a while to adjust to having two fathers, though."

Will supplemented the facts. "I don't want to replace your dad, in any way. I don't want to interrupt that relationship. Maybe I could be your friend Will who's a writer."

Seamus' lawyer was surprisingly on time. Will had met him a few times at the office. "Hey, Will... you sure you're okay... in your right mind and all?"

"Yeah, Tim, I'm good. Got that contract?"

Amy looked concerned. "Can I see? I'm good with contracts." Tim handed her the papers, and she read quickly. "This is actually quite good. Most publishers and some agents would take more. Very clear, clean. Good work. Tell your writer I like the style. You can go ahead and sign this. I can notarize."

Tim took the contract back. "Your new lawyer?"

Will realized that he hadn't introduced anyone. As he was signing, he made up for the oversight. "This is Lane, who I knew in college, and her daughter Amy, who found me in the park."

Tim shook Amy's hand first. "Thank you a thousand times. Life would be just a sad thing without my pal here." Looking at Lane, he smiled more deeply. "You wouldn't be a single lady, would you?" Lane shook her head.

Will shook his head. "Neither is his wife, the one with the three kids."

"Awww, a guy can dream a little, can't he? If you're going to be like that I'll take my papers and go back to my dingy office where I slave daily to provide food and shelter for my poor family."

Lane smiled. "You sure he's not a writer too?"

Tim volleyed back. "No time, dear lady. This one throws three books a year at us, and we have seven other patients to deal with. The boss, Seamus, won't let anybody else work with Will's manuscripts, and he approves everything we send to publishers."

Jack came bursting in, big grin on his face. "Aidan! I know who you are! You're William MacLeish, greeting card writer and designer! One of my gallery contacts got your Christmas card last year!" He looked around the room. "What? Nobody reacts?"

Amy filled him in. "The man's memory came back."

Will looked a little guilty. "Apparently not everything. I had forgotten about the cards. Now that you mention it, I've done them the last three years. That sketch you saw, Jack, was last year's Christmas card."

The phone rang again. Amy answered, sounding rather monotone. "Hello?... oh yes, hi... you did? That's great. Dinner Monday? Sure. Love it... oh, nothing to worry about. Just some family stuff to absorb. See you Monday." Then she announced to the room "Paul says they know who your attackers were, and they're in the process of picking them up. Since you couldn't ID them, Paul is going to try for a confession. They had been bragging about it. Shouldn't be too hard."

To Will "I guess you'll want to get back to your life now, huh?"

Will had another idea. "If it's okay with you, I'd like to stay, at least tonight. It's more comfortable here than in my apartment alone."

That cheered her up a bit. "Oh, goodness, look at the time. Has everybody eaten?" The consensus was no. "So let's ask the cook. What's for dinner?"

Will had a plan. "Amy's going to make Linguine Carbonara."

"I'm what?" Amy's eyes went wide.

"That's right. I'll be right beside you, it'll turn out perfect."

"Aagh! Mom, he's making me cook!"

Lane hugged her daughter. "Congratulations."

Will made an announcement. "Dinner in about twenty minutes. Meanwhile, if someone would open that lovely box of red and set the table, the two of us will disappear to the stove and work some magic."

Twenty two minutes later, dinner was served. Everyone very much enjoyed the food and the company. At 10:30, Amy called a cab for Lane, and ushered Jack back to his place. "I know it's not a work day tomorrow, but some of us need to sleep anyway."

Once everyone else had gone, she had something to say. "Thanks for staying. Your sudden absence will be a loss. I've gotten used to having you here."

"Hey, it's not like you're losing me. I just won't be sleeping here. Want to come with on some errands tomorrow? I'm walking well enough to get from a cab into a store and back to the cab, and I'd appreciate the company."

Amy smiled her more relaxed smile, the one Will had gotten used to. "Sure. Shopping with my other dad. Let's do that." She wandered off toward bed after giving him a big hug. "I'm glad I don't have to lose you completely... who else is going to solve cases for me? Seventy books, huh?"

As they started their morning, Will announced the itinerary. "First to my agent, to pick up some money, then to our shopping stops. Picking up a birthday present for a good neighbor, and a wedding gift for someone I still think of as an overly charming five-year-old." They called a cab, finished their cinnamon toast and kippers, and were off.

Seamus was an odd man, by Will's impression. Married with two children, he had kept his first efficiency apartment from when he and Will had moved to New York, and now used it as an office. When Will and Amy came through the door, his face lit up. "Dude! You finally dating? She's a little young for you, and way out of your league, but kudos." Aside, to Amy "Don't worry, whatever hold he has on you, I'll help you escape."

Amy picked right up on the joke. Batting her eyes, she played the ingénue. "But good sir, why would I escape the arms of the best daddy a girl could have?"

Seamus was stymied. "Okay, Will... I want to know what college campus you kidnapped her from, and what kind of drugs you're feeding her."

Will laughed, then Seamus. "No such skullduggery. Amy is the one who found me on a bench in the park. She let me stay at her place until I got my memory back. She saved me."

Amy delivered the coup de grace of this introduction. "Then he met my mom, remembered things, and found out he's my biological father."

It took a minute for that to sink in, during which Seamus sat down. "Your daughter..."

Will grinned. "Yup. And I couldn't be more proud. She's compassionate, literate it turns out her favorite book is our first, and grab me a hardback of that when you can, plus she's smart. Amy's a lawyer."

"Sheesh. But you didn't have all the "fun" of helping her grow up."

"Yeah, well... one can't have everything. Hey, do I still have that credit card around here somewhere?"

Seamus thought about that. "Yeah, but you locked it out. We'll have to see if you can unlock it."

"I'm feeling like a shopping spree. They should be glad to see some action."

"Shopping spree? What has this girl done to you? This guy spends about twenty dollars a month, over utilities and groceries. What are you going to spree on?"

"First, the camera store, then a gift for Amy's mom, and one for Amy, and a wedding present for a friend."

"Whoa. The camera store you like is closed Saturday, remember?"

"Aw crud, you're right. Well, we can get the rest of the stuff and go there tomorrow."

"Right. Let's get that card activated." It only took five minutes to activate the card, and they were off. First stop, Tiffany.

As they were leaving, Will turned to Seamus. "I want to go ahead with that idea we talked about, dumping the pseudonyms."

"I was hoping you had forgotten."

"Just look into it, please... find out what it'll take? Please?"

"For you, anything. I'll let you know.

Amy hadn't been in the Tiffany store before, so was busy for a few seconds being stunned. "Hey, Amy could you find a vase, something upscale, maybe two colors twisted together?" She could tell that she was being assigned to another department so he could find her a gift, but wasn't bothered by it. She resolved to find the best wedding vase ever.

Meanwhile, Will strode over to necklaces. "Hi, I'm looking for a gift for a mother and daughter, something that says 'I'm sorry I haven't been there'. They both go for simple, classy pieces. Understated."

The salesman smiled. "We have a number of mother-daughter sets which may be satisfactory. Any preference of metals, stones, price?"

Will thought about it. "Not really. The right pieces are more important."

"Does the mother have the same coloring as the young lady you came in with?"

Astounded at the man's powers of observation, Will answered "Yes"

"Oh good. I think I have the right set. Right this way, sir." He led the way to a case full of necklace sets. "Something like this, perhaps?"

Will looked over the choices, churning them over in his mind. Not right, no, almost, not quite...Eureka! He pointed. "That one."

"Excellent choice, sir. This will go with the ladies' coloring very well."

"Is there anything that wouldn't?"

"Certainly, sir. Most diamonds would almost disappear, rubies would seem too red. With the Black Hills Gold mesh and a single emerald, these are the coloring I recommend. You could get away with the Fire Opal set, but they are drops. The one you selected has the stone attached to the gold mesh, as to seem like it is floating there."

Will was very satisfied. "Okay, I'll take them. They come in separate boxes, right?"

"Yes sir. That's $25,750."

"Good. I want to surprise the daughter. She's not expecting anything." He handed the man his card.

"Wonderful surprise, sir. If you'll sign here, and face the camera a moment."

Will signed the machine and smiled for the camera. He remembered that when he got the card there was a picture involved. He grabbed his receipt and bag and was off toward Amy. He turned back to the salesman. "Thanks. This really is exactly what I wanted."

Then he went over to Amy. "So, you find anything?"

Amy seemed torn. "I can't decide between these two." She pointed out two similar vases.

"May I help?" The salesperson swept over to them, her long skirt giving her the illusion of floating.

Will confessed "We need a wedding gift. I know these people like cut flowers."

"A young couple?"

"Yes. I've known the girl since she was five."

"Excellent. Is there anything she's attracted to, visually?"

Will searched his memory. "Oriental, I guess. She's the only person I know with a hand-painted kimono, and a jade dragon. The dragon is a reproduction from the museum."

"I might have just the thing." She led the way to the porcelain vases. "This might be of interest. It's a wedding scene." She took a vase off the shelf.

"It's rectangular…"

"Yes. With the wedding scene all the way around, hand carved and painted, and there are dividers inside, to hold five individual blooms if desired."

Amy was impressed. "Almost makes me want to get married. The whole scene looks so happy."

Will grinned. "Chinese, by the look of it."

"Actually, this vase is American. An artist in North Carolina makes them. It's one of a kind, so no-one else will ever have the same one."

Will nodded. "That's what we want. I'll take it."

"That's $3,500, sir, plus tax."

Amy looked like she was about to say no, but Will handed over the card. Amy stared at him. "What are you, made of money?"

"No, just that this girl will, I believe, only marry once, and she's very very happy. She's important to me, she's the daughter of a good friend. The two of them kept me out of the rabbit hole a couple times."

"Women just want to save you, don't they?"

"Lucky for me, a few do. Does your mom have a favorite artist?"

Amy was at a loss. "Not sure. She has a couple posters in nice frames...Monet, Van Gogh..."

"Perfect! Let's go get mom some art!" He asked the sales woman. "Do you know where I could find a Mary Cassatt painting in town?"

The woman's eyed widened. "Not off the top of my head, Mr. MacLeish, but I know someone who will. I'll be right back."

The older man who returned with her was dressed in an older English style. "I understand that you are interested in Mary Cassatt."

"Yes. I know someone who would appreciate one of her paintings."

"Well, sir, that will be quite an investment."

"Yes. Well worth it."

"As it happens, there is a gallery that has recently acquired three of this artist's works. Havens Gallery on 63rd. Allow me to offer my card, and call in advance. They are not open to the public today, but I am sure that an appointment could be arranged."

Will took the card. "Thank you c'est tres gentile."

"C'est rien, monsieur." The English stiff upper lip softened into a smile. He held up a finger, as a sign to wait. A few minutes later, he came back, still smiling. "You are expected, Mister Macleish. A pleasure to be of service."

Outside, the cab driver was surprised. "More shopping?"

"Yes indeed. Havens Gallery on 63rd." When Will and Amy walked out of the gallery with what was obviously a wrapped painting, the cabby grinned. "A success, I guess."

"Sure was. Now to home for lunch. After this, peanut butter and jelly, with chips." Will couldn't contain the big happy smile. Amy was a little stunned.

"No limit on the card?"

"True. The bill goes to my bank, they confirm, and payment is made. So, no interest charged, either."

"Oh God... I thought there was no money in being a writer."

Will giggled. "There isn't, unless your agent sells a tenth of your work to be turned into movies."

....

Lane joined them for a late lunch at Amy's, bringing her friends along. The menu changed from peanut butter and jelly to small chef's salads with Parmesan shavings. Once everyone had eaten, Will stood to make a presentation.

"Lane, I couldn't be happier that we have reconnected after all this time. We went shopping this morning, and I got you a present." He handed her the pale blue box. "That's for all the birthdays I've missed."

Lane opened the box, and the case. She started shaking when she saw the contents. "But... I can't... I..."

Will was ready for this. "It's only a bauble. I thought that on you, it could come to life." He draped the necklace on and secured the clasp.

"Will... it's real, isn't it?"

"Of course. And I guessed right. Looks beautiful on you."

Amy was impressed all over again. "Gosh, mom... that's fantastic. Wish I could have something like that.'

Will reached back into his Tiffany's shopping bag and handed her the box. "Now you do." A matching necklace, a touch lighter, with a smaller stone. Both women started crying. Will admonished them. "Maybe you could save that for the big present. Lane, this is to celebrate your wedding."

He slid the sturdy cardboard box in front of a chair, slipped out the bubble-wrapped package, removed the bubble wrap and the acid-free tissue paper. Putting all that aside, he revealed the prize, leaning it on the chair.

Amy started crying first. Lane looked and smiled. "That's gorgeous. I've never seen a print of that..."

Amy had to tell her. "Mom, that's not a print. It's an original. Look closer."

Lane went over to the painting, noticing that the paint had texture. She put up her hand and almost touched it, then melted backwards, fainting. Her friends helped her to the couch.

Will asked Amy "Does she do this all the time?"

Amy shrugged. "Only around you, I guess." She nudged him playfully.

When Lane came back around, she was protesting. "Will, really... I can't accept..."

"Sure you can. Mother and daughter will keep your heart warm while your little girl goes about her grown-up life. I want you to have something beautiful, for those gray, cold times life throws at us all." Lane hugged him, for a long time.

Amy thought of something. "Hey, you ladies have dinner and a show to get to..."

Lane responded. "Not for a couple hours. I want to stare at this for a while. Can we come back after the show?"

"Sure, mom... come ahead. I'll have a pot of coffee waiting."

Will added "And streusel." The group sat silent for the next hour, soaking up the emotional content. When they left for dinner, Will asked "Are you up for some more shopping tomorrow morning?"

Amy sat next to him on the couch, leaning against him gently. "Sure."

Sunday morning in the camera store, Will was explaining to the clerk. "A friend of mine read a story about a man who had a Leica, just the camera and lens, for forty years. He took pictures of his family. A famous photographer saw his work and showed it to everyone..."

The clerk's lightbulb lit up. "The Book of George"! I read that last year, then everybody I know read it. Thing is, the best of the Leica community is really like that. Support from all over the world."

"Good story. Well, she took it seriously, and wants that kind of connection to a camera, and to a community. She's saving to buy the digital rangefinder, but she's only up to $500. I thought I would accelerate things. I'm pretty sure she wants the black one. And just the 50mm lens. That's all manual control, right? She wants that."

"Yes, sir. Comes with the normal lens, case and a strap. Would you like any accessories?"

"Definitely. Flash, extra battery, small bag. And I think she'll need a computer and new software to handle the pictures. Hers slows down once an image gets bigger, you know, if you play with it enough."

The clerk nodded. "Know exactly what you mean, and we definitely have the solution. Just a sec." He dialed an extension on the phone. "Hey, Norm... could you bring that computer and software package we have been selling so much of over to the Leica counter? Thanks." He went about pulling out the accessories. It took Norm a couple minutes to arrive. "Are you sure you don't want some lenses?"

Will shook his head. "No, she wanted to keep it simple. Even the flash is my idea. How much is that?"

The clerk did some quick addition on a calculator. "10,600, with tax."

Will looked around for Amy, saw her at another counter. "Hold on." He walked over to her. "Hey there. Find something you like?"

"Sure. This little one would be handy. Twice the megapixels of my phone, and an actual optical zoom. Plus, it fits in a pocket or purse." She asked the salesperson. "How much for one of these?"

"Three twenty, miss."

Will pointed to himself and rubbed his fingers together while Amy went to take out her wallet. "Oh, no, I am mistaken. Apparently it's free."

"Will, you don't get to buy everything." She punched him playfully and handed the salesperson her card, scowling at her would-be benefactor. He headed back to his own purchase, where the young man behind the counter was about to think he had lost a sale. "Okay, let's go with that deal for the birthday gift, plus I think I'll give her some competition. I've been doing some reading. I would like that same model, in silver with an extra 28mm lens, Metz flash big enough to do a wedding reception, small bag and software. Pretty sure my computer can handle it. How much?"

"Ummm... $15,600."

"Good. I'll take them. 24,400 total."

"Yes, sir. I'll throw in a lens cleaning kit and extra memory card with each. Plus, this little book that covers the basics. Mostly composition for beginners."

"Cool." He handed the man his card. It took a few minutes to get everything out of the back room, so he wandered over to Amy. "Didn't mean to be overbearing or anything."

She smiled and hugged him with one arm. "Didn't mean to be defensive. I'm not used to somebody paying for so much, now that I have a job. Cool little stuff like this is fun to find and buy."

"Yeah I've been researching that birthday gift for about three months. It sounds like such fun I got myself one too. Hey, mom and the girls will be at your place to pick up the painting in about three hours. Can I tempt you to the last of the strudel?"

"Yes, sir."

"How about after that we spend a couple hours at my place and have a simple Sunday dinner there?"

"Ooh... I get to see the famous author's place. Probably the ultimate bachelor pad, right? Good thing I know you're not what mom would call a wolf. Sure, that sounds good. As long as I'm home and asleep around ten"

"Deal."

After an appropriately mushy goodbye to Lane, and promises all around to keep in close touch, the theatre group was off. "Come with me, young lady, and discover how a bachelor really lives." To the cabby "425 Broome."

When Will opened the door to what he had called 'a simple one bedroom, good for a couple overnights', Amy gasped.

Will called out "I'm home..." and a voice responded "Welcome back, Will. Who is your guest?" Amy was stunned. Will filled in. "This is Amy. She gets full resident clearance."

The voice came back. "Voice print for your guest, please."

Will whispered to Amy "Anything you might say entering a room, speak clearly."

"Hello the house!" Amy was amused.

"Voice print on file. Welcome, Amy."

Will spoke again. "Security system off, until I reactivate."

"Turning off."

Amy looked around. "I don't even see any speakers. I didn't know artificial intelligence had come so far."

"Mostly, it hasn't. I got a free beta trial, supposed to report any problems. So far, nothing. If anybody comes in and doesn't clear the voice print, the system locks the door and windows, calls the police, and turns on video surveillance. Now, any time you come the system will recognize you by image and voice. Like the décor?

"Holy sh... sugar, Batman... the living room is the size of my apartment! Plus, who's your interior designer?"

"What you're seeing is 85% of the place. Kitchen's over in the corner, and the bedroom won't fit a king-size. I do like the light, though. And everything in here is my choice. Some wine?"

Amy took up a position on the couch. "Sure. Any other surprises?"

"Not a one." Will poured two glasses. "So now that we have some time, I bet you have questions."

"You bet your bippee. Let's start with the real story, the full story between graduation day and becoming a full-time author." Amy looked at him as piercingly as she could.

Will handed her a glass. "Okay... I left the graduation ceremony as soon as I was off the stage and went home. My folks were still at the school. I grabbed some clothes and stuff, wrote them a letter of apology that I had let them down, and left. I bought a bus ticket as far west as I could, and wound up in St. Louis. I got some day work- I was only there about two weeks and I bought another bus ticket, wound up outside Phoenix.

"I got a job three days after I got there as a bartender. The owner let me stay in a room above the bar until I could get my own place. I guess I worked there about a year, then the bar got sold and I was unemployed. A couple months later, I got a job in construction and started drinking more. Two years later I found myself in a bar wondering if this was my life.

"One night I was wondering whether I could get to sleep without another drink, and this guy sits next to me. Says I look like he feels. I had seen him at the bar before, so nothing unusual. We started to tell stories while we worked our way through some more beer, and out of nowhere, he says 'I always wanted to be a literary agent. What did you want?'

"So I say 'You could be my agent... I wrote a few stories in school that were pretty good'. Things took off from there. He didn't believe me, so I typed up one of the stories I had written. The two of us polished it up, and he sold it. We struck a deal that I would keep writing, he would help polish, and we would split any income.

"After a while we had eight stories and *Thessalon* was born. That thing took off, it had a life of its own. So we kept going. The first couple years were slow, but eventually I got into a rhythm, and could write three books a year without too much trouble."

Amy had to ask. "So why the pseudonyms?"

"Seemed like a good idea at the time. If interest in one name, or genre went south, we would still have the other two. And I noticed that I wrote differently under each name. So that became my job and I kept at it. When Seamus told me he had sold the movie rights to my fifth mystery, I almost didn't believe him. Eighteen months later our percentage started showing up, and neither of us had to do anything else.

"So that's what I have done for twenty-seven years, how about you?"

Amy shook her head emphatically. "Not quite done with you yet. What about romance? You write it, how much have you lived it?"

"Oh. Let's see... once I asked a woman to marry me, we'd been together for two years. I might as well have asked her if she wanted to be shot in the head or heart. She literally stood up, without a word, and ran away. Then there's the two, no, three that made it through a couple months then left. Toss in a few first or second dates and you've got my love life. Guess I'm not very good or lucky in that department. I have a couple friends up in the countryside that help keep me sane. Your turn."

"More wine." Amy held up her glass, and Will walked off to fill it. "Let's start with high school. After Junior year, I felt broken. Lost. I told mom I needed a break, wanted to get a job. I worked at her school tutoring kids that were falling behind, or needed help.

"After that year, I decided that I would get through college as fast as possible, and be some kind of counsellor. I tested out of high school and went to college. I was studying Psychology, and met these two guys Charlie and Dave. Flaming brilliant. They were in Pre-Law. Eventually, I switched majors. The three of us helped one another through school, then through Law School. No time for romance. The guys both got married within six months of passing the Bar.

"I went to work for a little law practice, doing family and civil work, then the guys called me. They were working downtown, doing criminal and business work. They both recommended me, and I got the job working with them. The day I found you, we had just seen our work not only solve a case bot resolve it out of court. The boss was so happy we now work with him almost exclusively. And now I've met Paul."

Will grinned. "And how is our favorite detective?"

"Good. I still don't have a huge lot of time to pursue it, but there are possibilities there. He's a good guy."

"He thinks a lot of you, too."

"Nice."

Will had a thought. "Like some music?"

"Sure."

Will opened part of the wall. "Records on the left, CDs on the right, and there's an iPod in the middle. Sections say what kind of music is where. Guest's choice."

Amy sorted through some of the vinyl. "Wow. Really old blues. All kinds. I haven't heard anything from a turntable in years. Mind putting it on for me? Don't want to break anything."

Will felt like a party. "May I have this dance?"

Ten minutes later, they sat back down. "Do you like Gaspacho?"

Amy tilted her head. "Sure, if there's a nice rough bread with it."

"We can do that too. Let me set it up." He threw some things in a pot and kneaded some bread dough. "It'll be individual rolls instead of a loaf, that'll save time."

9:30 found them leaned back on the couch, listening to some Brahms. Amy's watch beeped three times. "Oh gosh... well, if I need to unwind, I know where to come. Right now it's home and asleep. Thank you. I'm amazed to know you." She headed toward the door.

"There's a car waiting at the front door, and the driver's ID is on your phone."

"You sneak. Arranged that while I was hypnotized, did you?"

"Nope. While making dinner."

Amy kissed his cheek. "See you, Will my friend who's a writer... see you soon and often."

"Yeah. This month, anyway. Then it's my turn to work."

Will listened to the rest of the Brahms, then toddled off to bed himself. Jane and Marisa wouldn't arrive with Harvey until noon.

3

Right on cue, Marisa called from the car. "We're about ten minutes away."

Will was delighted. "I'll be on the sidewalk. I got you a parking spot." He jogged down the stairs and onto the sidewalk. Beautiful, for a Monday. Sunshine, a little breeze. He was wrapped up in the spring experience when a horn woke him. He leaned over to the passenger's window. "Take the second right, go around to the back of the church, The guard is waiting for you." Harvey was about to come out over the young woman's head, so Will opened the rear door and grabbed the leash. Harvey pulled his favorite human toward a small tree.

The car took off, and Will and Harvey followed. By the time they arrived at the church, Jane and Marisa were walking toward them. "Lunch awaits, if you're hungry..."

"If! I had an English Muffin at six. But I want a hug first." Jane wasn't a fan of the drive, but she had made it several times. "Babe, it seems like it takes 15 or 20 minutes longer each time I come down."

"Yeah. That's why I don't drive. How you doing, Marisa, getting nervous about the wedding?"

Marisa, the talkative one. "Sure."

Will had the cure. "Let's eat!" The women turned to walk, the way he had come.

"Geez, mister M... you make the best sandwich and fries ever. Thanks." Marisa was back to talking. She had never gotten used to long drives, and hardly ever left the town she grew up in.

"So now it's presents time! One for the bride... sorry I didn't get it wrapped all pretty..." He handed Marisa the box.

"Ooh... that's some kinda beautiful, mister M... looks like a happy wedding." She turned the vase around and smiled broadly. "Thank you. That'll be great with some flowers in the living room."

Will probed a little. "So you know where you're going to live?"

"Sure do. Mace is going to take over his grandma's house. He's been doing work on it, and she's getting on in years, so we'll just live there."

"That's the white house with the big porch at the edge of town, right?"

Marisa grinned. "Yeah. Mace says once it gets a fresh coat of paint it'll look great."

"By the look of it, might take more than paint. How about I get Mace something as a wedding present, too."

"Like what?"

"Like some credit at the home store, so he can go in and get what he needs whenever he needs it, just go pick things up."

"Ooh... he might go crazy. I'll have to keep him from spending too much."

"I'll bet that won't be a problem. If you think he's worth marrying, I bet he's a good guy. I'll arrange for five thousand to start. That's enough for paint and a few brushes."

Marisa put down the vase and ran to hug Will. He was glad he could help. She had even more to say. "There's something else I was going to ask you for, for a wedding present..."

“What’s that?”

“Well, if it’s not too much, on top of what you’ve already given, I’d dearly love some pots and pans like you have. Mace’s grandma, well her stuff is kinda old and worn.”

Will grinned and kissed her forehead. “You got it, kid. Pots, pans and utensils too.”

“Thank you so much.” Will could tell by the way she mumbled it that she wasn’t thrilled about being Mace’s cook and housekeeper.

“And now for the momma... the birthday girl.” He went into the bedroom and came back out with a box the right size for a toaster oven. “I didn’t wrap this one either.”

Jane set the box down and peeked inside, closing it back up immediately. “I’m gonna cry, aren’t I?”

Will grinned. “Maybe a little.” He handed her the tissues.

Jane took a deep breath and opened the box again. “Oh my god. Tell me this is something else in a camera box.”

“Nope. You liked that story so much I thought you’d enjoy it. Has more features than the old film camera in the story. What else is there?” Jane reached in and pulled out the computer and software.

“Thing about digital cameras, the computer is their darkroom. They need it. And I checked, Romer’s Portrait Shop will make any prints you want.” Sure enough, Jane was crying.

“A camera AND a computer AND software? Will, I can’t...”

Will was ready for this. “Of course you can. Number one, you didn’t ask for anything. Two, I could have gone cheaper, but number three my best actual longtime friend should have one thing that’s the best of its kind. Besides, who else can I have a contest with?”

Jane looked up. “Contest?”

"Yeah. To see who gets the better pictures. I got myself one, too." He took his new camera out of a drawer. "It looked so good, so user-friendly when the guy was showing it to me, I couldn't resist."

It took the two of them about 45 minutes to get the cameras set up and Jane's computer accepting photos for editing. Jane then confessed her other motive for driving down. "I want to spend a day at MOMA. Bringing Harvey was my excuse."

"Mind some company?"

"Not at all. I might sit there and contemplate things for a couple hours."

"Cool. Want to go now, or rest up and go tomorrow?"

"Rest up, I guess."

"Good. I'll get us a car and driver." Will went to the phone.

"Do they have a gift shop?" Marisa, always willing to shop.

"Sure do, babe. Bet some things are even under a thousand dollars.

When Will got back to them, he seemed a little subdued. "Car service will pick us up here at ten, and we call whenever we're ready to come back. Hey, want to take our cameras for a walk around the neighborhood?"

It seemed like a cheerful thing to do. "Sure. Anything wrong?"

"Nah, not wrong. I keep thinking what would have happened if Amy hadn't found me in the park. The hospital said I was on my way to gone." Will remembered the first reminder in the manual. "We have to remember about the lens cap."

Jane nudged him. They picked up the cameras and were off. Marisa had Harvey in her lap and decided not to go with. Harvey lifted his head for a moment then went back to his nap.

Out on the street, Will and Jane headed toward the church. Architecture seemed like a good first subject matter. Jane confided in her friend. "Morris is getting a little jealous of the time I spend down here. I told him he could come, but he doesn't even like to think of a place the size of New York City. And just before we left, he said something about 'Have fun with your rich boyfriend', and that kind of pissed me off. He's my husband for gods sake. Thirty five years I've been taking care of him, helping with the farm, and I get jealousy?"

Will took a couple pictures of the stonework. "At least he's a nice guy. This the first he's said anything about it?"

"Yeah. There were a couple little digs last time I came down."

Will was silent a moment. "Often enough, guys don't believe a woman will stay with them. I've heard a few men, married or not, say something like that. Maybe when you get back, make a point of saying that you're not going anywhere. He goes out hunting, right? Takes a week in deer season, right?"

"Yeah."

"Show him that a trip down here is like that. Maybe bring him something back. I bet that solves it. He might need an occasional booster on the continuing nature of the relationship."

Jane took a picture of a tree blooming against the stone wall of the church, with part of a stained glass window off to one side. Will was impressed. "Jeez, you caught that one just right. Without the window it wouldn't be half as interesting. Looks like I have to catch up."

One picture led to another, and they wandered down the street, around some corners, in and out of some shops and stopped at a tiny park. Some children were playing, so Will asked the nearest mother if he and Jane could test out their cameras taking pictures of them. A few minutes later, they shared their results.

"Oh... that one. Can you send me a copy?" Mom was impressed. Jane had won this challenge. With the promise of an e-mail, Will and Jane headed back to the apartment.

Taking a different route back to the apartment, they came to one of those tiny galleries with a drawing and a small sculpture in the window. A Mills Galerie. Stopping in, they looked around. One piece caught Jane's attention, a pen-and-ink of a tired cowboy on a horse. "Hey Will... come see this."

Will came away from an abstract he was staring at. "Wow. That's nice."

Jane filled him in. "Morris is way into Westerns on TV. I think he can imagine himself as a cowboy. Bet he'd love this."

Will agreed. "You thinking of this as a souvenir?"

"Yeah. $50 unframed, I can get a frame back home..."

"Or Morris can make one."

"Oh yeah or Morris can make one." To the sole employee "I'll take this one."

On their way out of the gallery, Jane saw something. "Hey Will... isn't that your agent?"

"Where?"

"Straight across the street, with the cute blond."

Will looked. "Maybe..." He took a picture. "Yeah, I think so." The man across the street hugged the blonde, a long hug, and they walked off together

When they got back to Will's place, Marisa was playing tag with Harvey. Jane observed "It's amazing. They can run around at full speed and not knock anything over. Hey, Marisa, you think dad would like this?"

She looked at the cowboy and smiled. "I don't know anybody who wouldn't." Jane put it back in the box.

"Anybody else want an iced tea?" Marisa was pouring.

"Oh yeah. Not all that hot outside, but we did some walking."

Once everyone was ensconced with their drink, Marisa asked "Mister M, I sure would like to have a shelf or two of books I wrote... you think I could be a writer? Maybe not like you, but a few extra bucks in the household budget?"

Will thought about that a minute. "Sure. One thing about being a writer is that almost anybody can do it. All you need is a story to tell and a good way to tell it. Have you ever written fiction? I guess that's what you're talking about."

Marisa turned shy. "Just in school, but people liked them."

"Well that's enough to start with. How about you type up a couple stories. Short stories are a good way to start, it's more like you're telling a friend the story. I might have some suggestions, but if I like them I can send them on to my agent. He does all my editing and he's really good. Never know, might be more than a few dollars in it."

"Gee thanks mister M. How big should a short story be?"

"Oh, anything from two to forty pages. Depends on the story. A little practice and you get a feel for which ones could be longer."

"Cool. Are you really spending a month down here?"

"Yup. Getting to know my daughter."

"Cool. I'll have two or three stories you can read by then."

"Deal."

Jane wondered "Is there anything you won't do for somebody?"

Will laughed. "For family, like yours, or Amy or Lane... very little. I refuse to shoot people, steal anything or be a sourpuss, but that's just me being me in the world. Most other stuff is available to at least talk about."

Jane walked over and kissed his cheek.

Will reminded them "You two get the queen-size bed, I'll take the sofa."

"I always feel guilty displacing you."

Will assured her. "I got that sofa because it's comfortable to sleep on. No guilt available."

After a satisfying but uneventful visit to the Museum of Modern Art the next day, the group headed home. Marisa seemed down about something. "I got so wound up seeing the real paintings I forgot that I wanted to get some postcards to put in frames in the house when we move in."

Will had a solution. He told the driver "Houston, a block east of Broadway." To Marisa "Mom and I found a sweet little shop yesterday, and I think they have postcards." Marisa cheered up.

At the shop, the proprietor recognized them immediately. "Back for some more prints?" His eyebrows lifted hopefully.

Will responded, shaking his head. "No, but I think I saw some postcards of paintings in the back yesterday."

"Hmmm... postcards... oh, yeah. Anything specific?"

Marisa filled him in. "I'm getting married in a couple months. I'd like to get a bunch, put them in a frame together to decorate the house."

"Oh yeah. I've seen people do that. The ones I have are great for that. They're a little bigger." He led the way to the back, and pulled out a bunch of small boxes. "Afraid I overinvested. I got a dozen each of two dozen paintings." He opened all the boxes. "They're $2.00 each, I can give you a discount for a dozen."

Marisa looked carefully at each one. "I want them all. One of each."

The man must have been the owner. He was very happy at the thought of the sale. "Let's see... twenty four at two dollars is forty eight... how about thirty eight?"

Marisa looked in her wallet. "I might not have the tax."

Jane stepped in. "I'll take a set too. They're gorgeous. Way better than most postcards. Let this be a small wedding present. Two sets, and I know I can cover the taxes."

The man turned to Will. "How about you, sir? This makes you the only one of your party who hasn't bought something."

Will tilted his head and smiled at the man. He enjoyed a unique sales schpeel. "Actually, I saw a black cat statue yesterday that might be nice."

"Oh... the obsidian. There are two, one sitting up straight, one sleeping." He pulled them down and put them on a box. "One of a kind. Hard thing to shape this stone, it keeps wanting to shear. I've never seen obsidian this size. The artist also does these shapes in a dark jade."

Will didn't seem to have heard that last part. "One keeping watch over the other. How much?"

The man squinted at Will. "I was thinking $250 each, but it's a slow day except for you folks. How about $400 for the pair?"

Will smiled. "Done. I would have gone six if you had asked."

"Guess I'd rather move product than chase the dollar too hard."

"Good man. I'll make sure everyone knows you're here. See if we can get you some business. If they say Will sent them, go for the six."

The man grinned. "Glad to meet you, Will. I'm Albert Mills." He then went about looking for the right boxes for everything.

Will dismissed the car so the three of them could walk. On their way back to Will's, the group giggled and joked over their finds, wondering if they should become art dealers. As they got out of their hired car, Jane heard a car accelerating behind them. She turned to look and let out a little squeak of alarm.

Will looked, and grabbed both women, pulling them to the space between two parked cars. The large sedan on the sidewalk kept accelerating, and sideswiped some of the cars as it passed them. It sped away as quickly as a car can go in Manhattan.

The doorman of a nearby building had seen the drama, and yelled "Hey, you folks okay? I called 911." Will gave him a thumbs up.

Will turned to his guests. "This kind of thing really doesn't happen. You both okay? We should stick around a while, the police will need to hear what happened."

Jane hugged him, then held his hand. She couldn't even think of letting go. "Thank you. I froze. Marisa, you okay?"

Marisa was better at hiding fear. "Yeah. Somebody after you, Mister M?"

Will was surprised. A police car screeched to a stop beside them, yelling out the window "You okay? Which way did they go?"

Will yelled back "Fine. Turned left at the corner." He pointed. "Black, no plates." He couldn't be sure if they had heard the last bit.

The second car pulled up more calmly, and took a parking space. "You the folks with a car on the sidewalk?"

It only took the officer a few minutes to get everyone's information, and a clear picture of what happened. He handed Will a card. "If you see the car... anywhere... call me. Just in case we don't find it right away, you know..."

"Yes sir. Thanks." Will could tell that that officer wouldn't have believed them without the tire marks on the sidewalk. He doubted that there would be a quick end to the matter.

When the police car pulled away, Marisa turned to Jane. "Mom, I really want to go home now."

Jane took Will aside. "Look, I would stay another day, but this thing has me spooked too. I'll feel safer at home."

Will smiled at her. "Sure, I get it. Let's go get your stuff and get you on your way. You still have time to beat the evening rush." When they pulled out of the church parking lot, Will waved sadly. He didn't appreciate whoever that was who chased his friends away. He walked back slowly, trying to imagine who would try to hurt either his friends or himself.

Just inside his door, the security system challenged him. "Welcome back, Will. Please confirm." It took him a moment to remember his code phrase. "It was the best of times." The answer came back "Identity confirmed."

After dinner, Will was standing at the window, looking out into the fading light. His theory was that writing was a combination of a plan, an inspiration and a whole lot of typing. The current project was in the inspiration stage. The plan was to write a romance, set at the shore. He didn't know what shore, but he knew there had to be a tide, and the constant mumble of the waves.

Amy called. "Hi there… oh… what's the case?… oh sure… well come on over… we'll see what we can come up with… sure, hon. See you then." Will was left wondering what help his brilliant daughter could need. Something about corruption in the city government. Wait! That could key into his story. Even crooks fall in love. Sure, A crooked official falls in love, and winds up becoming the honest mayor. Cool. And, it gave him a way to see how corruption could work, and while he was thinking about it, maybe help Amy. A short brandy and a good night's sleep would help.

Amy showed up right on time, four in the afternoon. Once she identified herself to the security system, Will offered some wine. "Maybe later, or if I stay for dinner. I need a different perspective on this."

"So what's the problem? You said something about corruption at City Hall?"

"Right. Multiple whistleblowers have popped up, claiming corruption, malfeasance, misfeasance, theft in office… everything that would spend city money without getting anything. Case is so big the Attorney General has asked a few trusted friends with help identifying the sources and getting proof."

"Wow. And your boss…"

"Is one of the trusted friends. If we can even break some of this, the rest might stop on its own. The Attorney General is going to go hard on anybody we get proof against."

"Yeah. Make an example, and tell the rest you're coming for them next. Do you have any hints what departments? Going after the whole city government seems gargantuan."

"In fact, yes. We've been asked to look into two places the whistleblowers mentioned: office supplies, including purchase of computer systems, and Parks. Even with a limited scope, we can't get started. Both places submitted their budgets and expenditures for the last three years, but...

"But real corruption stays off the books. Accounting is the first place you want to avoid. Deals done in cash, or with verbal agreement. Like 'I'll give you this million dollar contract if you donate a hundred thousand to this weatherproofing program for the poor which coincidentally rehabs my house.'"

"Right, and maybe even more complex. In one case, the allegation is that it's nothing but free services being traded. That's even harder to track."

"Right. I put on my criminal thought cap last night, and came up with a couple things to look at. For purchase fraud, you need someone complicit at wherever you're buying from. That might be the most traceable thing. Maybe somebody a salesman who put more money in the bank than his salary and commissions. Might look into personal checks from anyone with purchase authority to anyone at the seller.

"For Parks, it's easy enough to say the lawn in Central Park was mowed three times a week but only do it once, billing for three. Tree services same way. Bill for three trees trimmed, but trim one. The hardest to fake are rest rooms and plowing the snow. But even then, with the rest rooms someone could charge for sanitizing but just take a high-pressure hose to the place and spray a little bleach around for effect."

Amy was stunned. "That's some criminal thought process you've got there. Are you sure all your money came from royalties and dividends?"

"Just to keep my street cred, no comment. My agent does all the money stuff."

"Yeah sure. So far, you've come up with more ideas in ten minutes than my office has in three days."

"You're welcome. I need some sugar. Want a turnover? I made blueberry, cherry and lemon cream."

After sugary treats (Amy fell for the lemon cream), Will had a proposal. "If you can give me a couple days, I'll make up some scenarios for fraud in a large city and we'll see if any of them might fit."

Amy's gratitude washed over her face and she sighed in relief. "Thank you. Afraid I'm only partly a criminal lawyer. I'm better at things with more evidence."

Will was consoling. "Aah, you'll get it. My first couple mysteries weren't my best work, but the more I tried, the more I looked into what people do, the better they got. This case could be some good experience. Say, your firm would have investigators, right?"

"Sure."

"Have them get the records of places computers were bought from by the city. Every record with a department name, or anyone's name in the department, for the last say five years. That ought to get you a place to start."

"To start what?"

"See if there are a lot of returns, or credits, or unexplained stuff."

"Oh. But won't that tip off the bad guys, if any? Remember, these are just allegations at this point."

"Yeah. Maybe get the bank records, instead of the company's. The Attorney General can tell them to keep it secret, at least temporarily."

"I'll look into that."

Will seemed done with the subject. "Can we be off the clock now?"

Amy hugged him. "Of course. How did things go with your friends from upstate?"

"Oh, one little car speeding up the sidewalk spoiled the vibe. They went home. I think Jane liked her present, and I bought a couple cats. Oh yeah, and Harvey is here."

"Harvey?"

Three feet of fluffy stood in the door to the bedroom. Will pointed. "Harvey. Come on, boy, say hello."

Harvey walked over to Amy. "Aroo" and sat, wagging his tail.

"Ooh… aren't you the smart one?" She stroked his head. "He's gorgeous, and has great manners. You could make a small fortune teaching human males the same thing."

Will got nosy. "How's things with Paul?"

"Good. I think I'll duck out on your pursuit of the subject and run home. I'll start working those couple ideas, and look forward to more." She kissed Will's cheek and was gone.

Will turned to Harvey. "See that? That's Amy. I helped make her." Harvey stood, tail still going.

Two days later, Will had accumulated fifteen scenarios for fraud, and thought he would deliver them in person. Dave recognized him right away. "Will! You're looking a lot better. Good to see you!" Will was lost. "Oh… I'm Dave. I was with Amy when she called the ambulance on you."

Will grinned broadly. "Oh yeah. She has your picture at her place. Herself, you and another friend."

"That's Charlie. The third Musketeer. So how are you doing? It's only been a couple weeks…"

"Yeah. I'm doing well. Won't be doing any boxing any time soon, but I'm walking and talking pretty much normal. Is Amy around?"

"Actually, no. She's out doing some research."

"Well, would you give her these? A few more ideas to consider."

"Sure."

"See ya. Maybe the four of us can have dinner some time"

4

Four days later, Will was in the middle of the second chapter. He had taken up the challenge of putting all of his 'defraud the local government' ideas in one novel. He had made up a city a quite a bit smaller than New York, just so he could keep track of things, and so some of the fraudsters could interfere with each others' plans.

Taking a break after fifteen pages of furious typing, he stood looking out the large window, and had a thought. "Hey, Harvey? Would you like to live here in the city instead of at the cabin? Lots more people to meet, less running. Feels like things are changing for me, the thought of having a daughter. Didn't expect how that changes what I think about."

Harvey trotted up to him, carrying a leash.

"Okay, don't stand still getting maudlin on your break, walk around outside. Good advice. Think I'll take the camera, see what there is in the neighborhood." Harvey wagged his tail so hard his rear feet almost left the floor.

Out the door and left along the street, Harvey watered an innocent sapling. "Hey, save some for the next one!" Will knew that the dog couldn't understand the words, but would somehow pick up the intent. Harvey was good at that, and at pulling Will toward the most interesting scents. They spent a full ten minutes enjoying the downwind evidence of a bakery, before Will lost his resolve and bought a dozen doughnuts.

Turning a corner, Will found out how much coordination it takes to operate the camera with one hand. Not possible. He tucked the box under one arm and managed to focus and click off a couple shots. Thank heaven the salesman had taken a few minutes to show him the basics.

Further along, Harvey started pulling, dragging his human helpless behind him, only stopping to sit next to a man enjoying the sunshine on the steps of a church.

Will thought to introduce himself. "Hi. Sorry about this, sometimes I walk him, sometimes he walks me. I'm Will, he's Harvey. Mind if we join you?"

The man grinned broadly and put down his coffee, extending his hand. "Not at all. You're very welcome. I was just thinking that I shouldn't be the only one enjoying what it feels like on these steps." He stroked Harvey's head, which produced a mighty wag at the other end. "Like some coffee?"

Will didn't know where it was going to come from, but couldn't wait to find out. "Sure. And we brought the donuts."

The man disappeared into the church, reappearing with another cup from the coffee shop in the next block, and a small bowl of water for Harvey. "I'm guessing you take it black, just a little sugar."

Will was delighted. "Good enough. You work here?"

The man blushed. "Yes, I guess you could call it that. Father Bob Carver, pastor."

"You seem young to be a pastor."

"That I am. 33, and the youngest parish priest in the Diocese."

Will opened the doughnuts. "There was a Father ... what was his name...Poslikowski...some years ago. Talked me into making cakes for a bake sale. We were walking down the street, and he calls out 'Can you bake?' and I say 'Yeah'. Wound up making a dozen cakes, all different. Not the big churchgoer, myself. I don't think of highly religious folk lazing about enjoying the sunshine."

Bob nodded his head. "Yeah. Father Poslikowski was offered another parish. As far as lazing about, I was composing a sermon. Something you don't see in the movies, or TV. If it helps, I'm just Bob, think of myself as the major d'omo. I manage the property, and get to live here, and tell people what's what."

"Okay... great spot you've found here, Bob. Appreciate you sharing it. Want another? We have to keep the chocolate ones away from my friend here."

Bob was amused. "Sure. We're eating the donuts to save the dog from them. I like the way you think, Will. You look familiar, like I've seen you before, only not with Harvey."

"Yeah, a couple blocks that way. We're taking a break from writing... I write novels and essays for a living, but I have a four hours at a time limit, so Harv here threatens the furniture so I'll stand up and walk."

"You married, Will?"

"No, not so lucky that way. You?'

"No, most women find out I'm a minister and think I would judge them. Actually, the reverse is true. Being a minister lets me not judge people, just want to enjoy them."

"For me, all I do, counting the last twenty-five years, is write. Word skills, got 'em. Romance skills not so much. Looking for families to convert?"

"No, just talking to you this couple minutes, I think you're a nice guy. Harvey helps with that impression. There's a single woman in the congregation who, I think, could use some nice guy time, if you're free."

Will didn't flinch. "Matchmaking?"

"Not exactly. More like... well... okay, yeah. Just meeting you, spending a little time, would be a good thing. Convince her there are good guys in the world, and they don't all turn away from her."

"Wow. What's been the problem?"

"Don't know."

"I don't expect to join up anytime soon..."

"Don't have to. We have a picnic next Sunday, in the park down the street, eleven to six, and we have all kinds of volunteer activities. No membership required."

Will thought about it a minute, noticing Harvey staring at him expectantly. "Oh heck, who am I to turn down a picnic? Guess I can bring my social crutch here?"

Bob stroked Harvey's head. "Always welcome."

"Okay then... we'll be there. Anything I can bring?"

"Nope. Our volunteers have it all set up."

"See you then. C'mon, Harvey... any more time in the sun I'll fall asleep. I've got a story to get back to. Bye, Bob."

When they got back to the apartment, the security system did its usual greeting "Welcome, Will." Will didn't know why, but the sound of the voice irritated him. "Security off."

Releasing Harvey from the leash, Will sat back at the computer, and quickly realized that he had lost both train of thought and desire to write, for the moment at least. Maybe some phone calls.

"Hey, Seamus, where are we on dumping the pseudonyms?...Yeah? Great. How about tomorrow morning?... Sure. See you then, bye." Gosh, that was easy. The thought of his own name on all those books was at once exhilarating and intimidating. Would he now have to autograph a million volumes? Should he put a picture on the back, with a biography?

He imagined the bio. 'Will MacLeish has done nothing but write for the last 25 years. Before that isn't important." Not strictly true, but not so much a lie, either. Maybe no picture and no bio for now.

Second call: Lane. "Hi there, it's your author. Is there a great time for me to talk to your class?... Right... Videoconference? I'm more convincing in person... sure, yeah... well, I have a writing exercise I could run through with them... maybe take half an hour... starts with a three word sentence, like 'John walked home." Then you add a word, then another, then another.

As the sentence gets more complex, it becomes the seed of a story. Right....Next Tuesday? Sure, I can do that. I'll be at the school at ten. Great. This will be my very first public appearance as a writer... oh yeah that's right I haven't told people... I'm coming out from behind the pseudonyms. There will be an announcement on the websites... right... See you Tuesday. It'll be fun. See you then."

Turning away from the phone, he noticed Harvey. "Oh gosh, Harv... I forgot to ask if I could bring you. That's okay, I'll send an e-mail later. Next victim, Amy."

"Hey, Amy... free for dinner or something tonight?...Tomorrow night, sure. In or out?... Love to: plain or fancy?... Okay, meat, potato, peas. Pudding for dessert... no pudding, cake instead? Sure, I can do that. How about six thirty? Great, see you then."

"Hey Harv..." his voice became very animated "...Amy's coming!" Harvey stood up and looked at the door. "Tomorrow, for dinner." Harvey consoled himself by snuggling at one end of the sofa.

"Okay... one more thing... the phone is going to ring." Will knew that Harvey wasn't listening. "Security... unsubscribe." The light went out on the security keypad. Will knew that it was only a matter of minutes before the monitoring company would call to try to talk him out of discontinuing the service. He poured himself a coffee.

Sure enough, at the four minute mark, the phone rang. "Hello... this is he... yes, I did... don't want the constant interaction... guests having to sign in... having to tell the system when I'm cooking... right... right... might be perfect for someone else... when can you come uninstall?... Okay... oh... well that's nice of you... yes, that will be fine... how much would that cost, if I choose to continue... yes, okay... great. If I'm not here, the building manager has access. Thanks, bye."

All those phone calls had made him hungry. Will fixed himself a chef's salad. Tomorrow would be busy too, with Seamus in the morning and dinner for Amy and Paul later. Better make sure to make up a statement, and have the ingredients ready to cook.

5

The next morning at Seamus' office, Will was a little worried. "Hope nobody thinks I've been lying to them."

Seamus had a different perspective. "Look, you have never told them who their favorite author is. You haven't lied, except in the way great fiction writers do. This is just an opening up, and it'll expand interest in your work. You're a more interesting character than any of those you've invented. This announcement is, at this point, the right thing to do, especially if you're thinking to slow down a bit, maybe do something different. Besides, I've already arranged for translations and new covers"

Will smiled. "Sounds like you're more hyped about this even than I am."

"May be true. But then you haven't heard all the positive comments from the publisher, and my research team says people love this kind of thing, getting to know who wrote what they love to read."

"Okay, let's make an announcement."

Seamus had set up a little studio in his office. "You'll sit here at my desk and start, then I'll come in to back you up. This is so cool."

Will sat at the desk, staring into the camera directly opposite. When Seamus signaled him, he took a breath and started talking. "Hi, my name is William MacLeish. During the last twenty-five years I have been writing Mysteries, Romances and Essays under three pseudonyms. Those names are Ari Cantor, Yuri Ivanov, and L.S. DuPont.

"It was not my intention to mislead anyone, or to hide. I wanted to give each genre its own writer, with a unique voice. Writing under three separate names let me do just that. What I meant to do was provide good experiences for the readers.

"I have been thinking in the last year to slow down, write a little less, and maybe something different. I hope that all of you who have for so long patronized my writing will continue to do so under my real name."

Seamus stepped into the camera's frame. "Hello, I am Seamus Doyle. I have been Will's friend, agent, and editor for all the time he has been writing, and I assure you that what you have just heard is true. Will wanted you all to know who your favorite writer is in real life. There may be some more details to be had, but for now this is our announcement."

Will tacked on "So bless you all, and thank you." The camera operator flicked the camera off. "And we're out! Geez, you guys... that won't even need any editing. Perfect."

Seamus started the next step. "So get that to the translators first, and as soon as they're done we post it to all three author websites. Is that fourth website up and running?"

"Yes sir..."

Will was curious. "Fourth website?"

"Yeah Q&A. Fans can send in questions and we answer them."

"Oh. Good idea to centralize that. Hope nobody accesses it before the announcement."

"No worries, it's just a blank website still. After the announcement goes up, we'll put a Q&A link on the three sites, and have dialog box for people to ask questions on the fourth site. Easy Peasy."

"Cool. Feels a little anticlimactic."

"Wait for it... things will explode within a couple days."

"I think I'll go take a nap."

"Good idea. Get lots of rest. See ya, bud."

Amy and Paul arrived precisely on time. Will advised them before they were through the door "You don't have to identify yourselves, the security system is off."

Paul was curious. "Why's that?"

Will was a little sheepish. "Sometimes the machine is too much. The voice became irritating. So, we have some little appetizers while dinner finishes up... how's everybody's day been?"

Amy grabbed a tiny pastry and started. "Actually, it's been a great day. End of the day, we got word that seven people have been arrested in the corruption investigation, and a dozen more expected over the weekend. That's because of your scenarios. The boss says thank you."

Will was pleased. "Tell the boss he's welcome."

Paul didn't seem so pleased. "Will, maybe you can convince this hardheaded lawyer to back off a little. Everybody knows who's working that case, and I'm worried about some pushback from people whose efforts to make money we're trying to shut down. Some of these folks are kind of vindictive."

Will leaned forward. "You mean they might think that going after her would stop the investigation?"

"Maybe not even that much thought. Somebody's cousin could decide they're mad at this person who put their relative in jail. It seems like Amy and her boss are the face of this thing, and Dave and Charlie are more in the background. Even the rumors around the station have her identified, and the place she works."

"Hmmm..." Will looked over at Amy. "It might be prudent to get out of the spotlight..."

Amy was immediately opposed to the idea. "Hell no. This case is a career-maker. If I back off, I won't get a chance like this for years."

Will nodded. "I do know about following the demand, doing what is asked. Just be careful, huh? No walking alone in the park for a few weeks maybe."

Amy smiled at him. "My boss already has a car take all three of us home, and the driver is an ex-Marine son of a friend of his. We're quite safe. Everybody might know where I work, but not where I live. I'm very very careful."

Will looked at Paul sympathetically. "Looks like that's all we get." He looked at his watch. "Five minutes to Small House Salads! Prepare yourselves!"

After the main course, Paul took a phone call. "Yes… right… okay, I'll be there. Thanks, Captain."

Amy scowled slightly "Sounds like work."

"Yeah. Later next week I'm being loaned out to the gang unit. Some new group running around destroying drug labs, disrupting dealers, and going after prostitution, gambling and loan sharks. We figure the drug cartels will be sending soldiers to reclaim their territories."

Will was curious. "New gang setting up their own operations?"

Paul shook his head. "Not so far. There's a whole bunch of customers going into withdrawal already."

Amy guessed "Don't tell me there's a vigilante law and order gang now…"

"Not sure. They call themselves 'The Invisible Millions', and they have no identifying tattoo, style of dress or anything. A couple dozen show up to disrupt a small drug buy, then they disappear back into the populace. The challenge for us is to determine their motive, identify some of them, and control anything illegal they want to do."

Will sensed that it was time for dessert. "Let us eat cake, and wish you luck."

Amy agreed.

After spice cake with apple chunks, Paul exclaimed "Oh, man, Will, you're going to have to teach me to cook too. That was the perfect dinner. I'm not overfilled, but I won't be hungry, and it all tasted spectacular. Oh, and hey, I heard about your announcement. Real cool."

"What announcement?" Amy looked at Will.

"I revealed that it was me behind my three pseudonyms. Figured it was time to just be me."

Amy grinned at him. "Bet there's a big fuss... don't let it go to your head." A half hour later, when Harvey would let them, the happy couple left.

"There they go, Harv... my little girl and the nicest cop I ever met."

....

The picnic turned out to be a bigger deal than Will expected: about five acres of Central Park full of people, music, food and games. Among other things, some kind of Frisbee tournament wound through the crowd. It took him a couple minutes to find Father Bob and start winding through the throng toward him. Along the way, a few people started whispering and pointing at him, something Will had no experience with.

Bob saw him coming, and met Will with a big smile and a bigger handshake. "Be forewarned: your romances are a big hit in the community. There might be some requests to sign body parts. Come on... lets find Harriet." Apparently Harriet was the name of the woman Bob wanted him to meet. Following Bob through a crowd wasn't the easiest thing Will had ever done. It was a surprise when he finally stopped, facing a woman Will would have called gorgeous.

"Will MacLeish, meet Harriet Consuela Meron."

She looked straight into Will's eyes and moved to shake his hand. "Hi, Will."

Will had been expecting to meet someone very different than the statuesque, graceful young woman with the hypnotic eyes that stood before him. He stammered a little. "Hi. Pleased to meet you."

Bob sensed that his job, for the moment, was done. "I'll leave you two in each other's care. Have to circulate." He walked off mercilessly.

"I'm sorry to stare..." Will quickly regained use of his social skills "...I just can't imagine any man ever walking away from you voluntarily."

Harriet chuckled. "Most guys don't really want Virgo women, especially not Virgo with Leo rising."

Will spoke this language enough to know what she was talking about. "Oh, I think desire wouldn't be the problem. More like belief. They don't believe you could stay with them. Of course, that belies a basic misunderstanding of both Virgo and Leo. Most guys just aren't used to having royalty want to do things for them. In this world, that's practically unheard of."

Harriet smiled. "So you know astrology. Impressive. Tell me about you... Bob says you're a writer. Fiction, right?"

They started walking as he talked. "Yeah. Romances, Mysteries, and Short Stories. That's about all I've done for a long time."

"No wife, family?"

"Nope... just writing. Apparently I write slowly. Actually, I just gave my agent the fifty-seventh book a couple weeks ago."

Her eyes widened. "Wow. I must have read some of your work. I tend to curl up with a book when I can. So what's your sign, mister Will MacLeish?"

He blushed a little. "Aquarius, Taurus rising."

"Holy smoke. And no conniving wench has trapped you yet!"

"Yeah, must be the writing. I'm a little monastic when I work, and that's been most of the time. Tried to have a relationship some time back... she got lonely." By this time, Harriet was holding his arm, engrossed. "Would you like some of this food I'm smelling from every direction? I had breakfast, but the scents are making me hungry again."

"Sure. Samples from each truck would be fun." By the time they tasted all the different foods, participated in the egg race and some carnival games, it was six o'clock, and Bob was trying to tell people the fair was over. Most of the crowd wasn't listening, and the food trucks wouldn't shut down until they ran out of food. Will had a good idea. "Want to go get an actual meal? Nibbling all day just doesn't fill me up. There's a great steak place down the block."

"Sure. Mind if my sons come?"

"Sons?"

"Yeah. Jorge is twelve, Manuel is fourteen. We'll have to guard our plates, they'll eat everything in sight." She held her breath, hoping he wouldn't run.

"Sure. I think this place will refill their plates if they want more... bring 'em on. I'll just drop Harvey back at home and we're off."

Bob came along as Will was walking away. "Hey there. How's it going?"

"Great. Were going out to dinner." Will wondered if he had been under surveillance the whole afternoon. "I'm just taking Harvey home first."

"Maybe I can save you the trip. Mind if I borrow Harvey while you have dinner?"

"Sure, but for what?"

"Receipts from the fair. It's a fund-raiser after all. I'd feel a little better with company walking to the night deposit."

Will chuckled at the thought of Harvey as a guard dog. "Sure, but you know he's a pet, not into security..."

Bob looked at Harvey. "But he's impressive. I'll bring one of the men, too."

Will shook his head. "Even if it's only a plot to keep me from interrupting a good time, okay. I'll pick him up after dinner."

"Great. C'mon, Harvey: let's go play in the finance tent."

Harriet let out the clearest, loudest whistle Will had ever heard, and two teens came running from the direction of the dance floor. "Mister William MacLeish, my sons Jorge and Manuel." The boys shook his hand.

Will's invitation "Would you like to have a sit-down dinner at a nearby steak place?" was met with an enthusiasm normally reserved for the arrival of someone from the sports or music world. Harriet smiled gently at the thought that these three guys might get along.

After dinner, and the boys had indeed gotten seconds, Manuel whispered something to his mother. She shoved him jokingly. "My precious and insensitive son wants to know if you're rich and where you live. You don't have to answer."

Will was amused by the word "rich". He never thought of himself that way. "Well, I'll say this: I have enough money to live on, and I have a one-bedroom in Soho and a house upstate." The boys were impressed.

"So you're cool, too." Jorge concluded. Mom laughed nervously.

"None of that, money or where you live, can make you cool as far as I'm concerned. Only the way you treat people. But yeah, it feels good to be a little successful."

Outside on the sidewalk, Harriet gave Will a slight hug and a kiss on the cheek. "We'll grab a cab from here. Thank you for dinner, and a nice afternoon. I'll have to commend Bob on his judgment of you. Spot on."

As Will walked away, he overheard one of the boys say "Mom... mom... you gotta get with this guy. He's real." Will didn't show that he had heard. The younger man in his own head was saying pretty much the same thing about Harriet.

Walking back to his place, Will was in a little bit of a fog. This was some of the social life he had imagined when he thought of writing less. Then his phone rang.

"Hey, Seamus, whassup?... Whoa, slow down... who wants what?... okay... fine, I'll be there. Does it have to be six in the morning? Yeah, okay okay... and what? I don't know, a book tour?... no, not for six months. Maybe weekends for three... sure, I can do that. How's that latest manuscript looking?... oh cool. See you in the morning." Will knew it was Seamus' job to promote him as a writer, but had a minor disagreement with doing national TV before he would normally wake up. And he would have to leave early to get to the studio on time.

On Tuesday morning, Will was at the studio at six. The pre-interview lasted half an hour, then it was the "Green Room", which was every color but green. There were other guests, some of whom were interesting or good conversationalists. At one point, someone ran down the hall calling out "The chef's not here! Who's the backup?"

Will wandered out into the hall. Seeing one of the producers, he mentioned "I can cook... French Onion Soup in four minutes, if you like." The producer raised an eyebrow. "Really?" Will assured him. "Sure. All it is is some beef stock, a couple onions, parsley and Worchester, topped with melted cheese and croutons. Very quick." The producer walked away, thinking.

Eventually, the show started. One of the political guests was up first, answering some issue in national policy. Then it was "Five minutes, Mr. MacLeish!" Will stood. He had sat enough for the moment.

Once in front of the camera, Will relaxed and answered the questions, smiling. Luckily, his explanation of the last 25 years seemed to satisfy the interviewer.

"At first, I wanted to try writing because my friend Seamus wanted to be a literary agent. I wanted to try it without the chance of being revealed as an incompetent who shouldn't be allowed to write.

"At first, I thought 'Thessalon" might sell a few copies, but be a flop in publication, so I'd just be another of the thousands of unsuccessful authors and nobody would notice.

"Then, a few months after it came out it was selling a thousand copies a month, and I was kinda stuck with a pseudonym. I wanted to try Mystery and Essays, and I thought nobody I knew of writes both, so I came up with two more pseudonyms. That way, if one writer failed it wouldn't effect the others. Only thing is, all three names have continued to have sales."

The interviewer was impressed. "By my count, that's twenty-three years. A lot of work. You're right up there with the most prolific writers in the country. How have you found time for a personal life?"

"Mostly, I haven't. I've just been working."

"I predict that there will be a number of fans willing to change that."

Will laughed "Completely unnecessary. My conversion from hermit to moderately social is well in progress."

"Well that's good. And thank you for talking with us this morning. The Director is telling me that you're our guest cook as well, so I'll hand you over to my co-anchors, in the kitchen. Stay tuned, folks, and we'll find out just how multi-talented William MacLeish is, after these messages."

After Will's demonstration of cooking skills, one of the anchors asked "So how does a bachelor wind up with such knife skills and such a quick cooking style? I've heard that French Onion Soup takes hours."

Will chuckled. "I have cooked for myself all this time. By the time I realize that I'm hungry, I need food quickly, and good food. I saw an episode of Julia Child's show, and she was making omelets. She made them fast, and encouraged the audience to cook boldly, and often. The only way to be good at this is experience. As far as the knife skills, I have so many tiny scars on my hands it's not funny. A little patience and carefulness with the cutlery goes a long way."

"Well that's certainly good advice. Last question: If you could share a meal with anyone living or dead, who would it be?"

A tear started to form in Will's eye, and he fought it back. "That would be my uncle George. From the time I was five, he gave me books for my birthday. I think the first one was Shakespeare's Sonnets. Beowulf for my eighth, Rumi for my tenth. Books that most people would consider out of reach for a person so young. I would want to show him that those books were perfect, and I still have every one of them. Unfortunately, he passed away when I was in college, before I started writing seriously."

"Well this has been a wonderful visit, please come back and talk to us again."

"Thank you very much, I had a great time."

"Next, our musical guest performs her song "On the Rocks" We'll be back after these messages."

Once the cameras were off. The producer came over. "Really. We'd like to have you back again, when you're available. The camera loves you, and I think our audience will too."

....

Wednesday came quickly, and Will was ready. He had hired a car and driver for the day. They arrived at the school at10:40. "Thanks. The driving is smooth as silk. I might be about an hour."

The driver nodded, and leaned his seat back.

Inside the Sound Beach School, Will found the reception desk. "Mrs. Leary is expecting me..."

The woman smiled. "Right this way, sir. Oh! You're that author... the one with the three pseudonyms!"

"Right. Lane and I went to college together, I thought her students would get a kick out of talking to an experienced author."

The woman relaxed. "Oh, I'm sure they will. Here we are." She knocked twice.

Lane opened the door. "These very well behaved students" (quite loudly, to remind the class) "are all very excited that you have taken the time to visit. Class, this is my friend, the celebrated author William MacLeish." A healthy round of applause ensued.

Will knew he had to take control right away, and remembered that he had liked doing much more than talking at that age. "Good morning young writers! I'm glad to meet you. Now, everybody's going to need a piece of paper and pen or pencil. He gave them a moment.

"The first thing we're going to do is write a very simple sentence, three or four words. I'll start two here on the board. This is one of the things I do when I don't know where to start with a story. Because absolutely anyone can come up with a three or four word sentence. Here are my two: 'Bob ran home' and 'The girl stood still' simple sentences.

"The second thing to do is to remind yourself of the five questions. I have them on a sign at my desk: Who, What, When, Where, Why. In order to turn your short sentence into a story, we'll be answering those questions. I recommend writing them in the margin of your paper.

"For the first of my stories, we already know Bob is the who. The reader wants to know why he ran home. Was he running away from or to something? I choose toward. Maybe somebody was going to make his favorite double chocolate cake. So I write 'He could almost taste mom's special chocolate birthday cake.'

"For my second story, the questions are two: why and who, as in who is she and why is she standing still? I choose that she is Dara, who knows that her bad little sister has a water balloon, but no accuracy in her throw. So I write 'Dara knew that Sue was too far away to be accurate, so her best chance of not getting hit with Sue's water balloon was stillness.' See? Answering questions is a lot easier than coming up with a whole plot out of thin air. Plus, you overcome the problem of the blank page. As you go on answering questions, more will come up.

"Right away, I want to know why is somebody making Bob's favorite cake, and why Dara doesn't ask her mother or father to tell Sue to stop with the water balloons. Sometimes I get so far into a story doing this that the momentum carries me right to the end. Every time I get to a pause, I ask the five questions and the answers take me farther toward the end of the story.

"How about if you start answering some questions, I'll come around and see how you're doing?" The students were too busy to notice that he had stopped talking. A trip around the room convinced him that he had lit a forest fire. He looked at Lane and shrugged.

Twenty minutes after he started, Will clapped his hands twice. All eyes turned to him. "Everybody close to a page of story?" Several held up two fingers. "Okay then. Now you're far enough in to answer a couple more questions. The first is 'What is your character's motivation? What do they want?' The second is 'What problems could keep them from getting what they want?'. The third is 'Are they going to get what they want?'.

"These answers will give the story a shape. They might help you decide who gets to tell the story. Is it Bob's dad, maybe Dara's little sister? Or are they both best told by an outside observer, the way I started both of my stories? If you decide these three things now, it's easy enough to go back and start from the beginning. It's only one page.

"So that's my idea that I wanted to share with you, it might make writing a little easier. Anyone want to share their work so far?" Four hands went up. After the four had read their work, Will gave them a compliment. "I can see that the future is in good hands, and I think that even if you don't all become professional writers, you can always have some fun with fiction. Thank you for your attention, and for sharing."

The students all hung their heads. One small voice came from the back row. "That's all? We were just starting to get somewhere. Half an hour isn't enough!" Agreement came from throughout the room. Lane thought fast, as teachers sometimes do. "Maybe, just maybe, we could invite Mr. MacLeish back in a couple weeks for another visit, when you have all had a chance to apply what you learned today. Remember, you will have homework meanwhile."

Even the dreaded h-word didn't dampen their enthusiasm. Cheers and applause greeted the thought. Lane turned to Will "What do you think, Mister M?"

Will looked around the room. "I'd be glad to."

"Can I lure you to a cafeteria lunch?"

Will could imagine the table getting crowded with eager questioners, but he agreed anyway. "Sure." Halfway through his small but delicious chef's salad, Will's phone rang.

"Hello... yes, of course. We're together, in Sound Beach, at Lane's school. It'll take a little while... we'll be there ASAP. Thanks, Paul" He leaned over to Lane and whispered in her ear. "We have to go. Amy's in the hospital. Paul says she'll be alright, but we should go. I have a car and driver."

Lane looked at him, alarmed, then stood and went to the principal, quietly advising him of the situation. Will and Lane resisted the temptation to run to the car. Once their seat belts clicked, Will gave the driver instructions. "We need to get to New York Presbyterian, East 70th by the river."

The driver got that this was urgent. "Yes sir... I know the place."

Will's phone rang again. "Hey, Paul... yeah? Good. We're on our way... oh sure... see you then."

"He says they won't release details on an individual patient because he's not family or the emergency contact, but they said nobody's got any fatal wounds, and a couple people only got grazed. Apparently, a group was going out to an early lunch, one man walked up behind them and started shooting into the group. He emptied the gun, dropped it and walked away. Seems like it wasn't attempted murder..."

Lane gained her voice. "So Amy's alive, probably been shot but not too serious..."

"Right." He put his arm around her.

At the hospital, Paul met them at reception. "Hi, I'm Paul DeVries. You must be Amy's mom. Hi, Will. They still won't tell me anything."

Lane went to the receptionist. "I'm Amy Leary's mother, Lane. Can somebody tell me her condition?" The receptionist called an extension.

"Go ahead up to the fourth floor, the nurse's station has the best information."

"Can my friends here come with? They're close connections of hers."

"Sure. I'll let them know you're on the way."

At the fourth floor, a nurse met the elevator. "Hi, Mrs. Leary. Right this way." She led the way to a room. Amy was sitting in a chair. "Hey, guys... you just missed the jello distribution. Could you tell them to let me leave?"

Lane hugged her. "Nothing too drastic?"

"Nah. I turned around when I heard the first shot, he wound up skimming bullets across my arm and my leg. A couple good bandages and some antibiotic cream for a week or two, I'll wind up with minor scars. My friend Charlie is in surgery to remove a bullet, but Dave got hit in the hand. They don't know if he'll regain full use. Only four people seriously hurt, five being treated and released. Will: you can talk people into things, get me out of here, wouldja?"

"We'll see what we can do." Will kissed her forehead. Paul pulled Will aside. "We don't know yet if this was a one-off or if there could be more shooters. I'm worried about these people being targets, since they were looking into corruption... Any way she can hide, maybe at your apartment for a couple weeks?"

Will nidded"I had pretty much the same thought on the way here. I have a couple ideas. Don't worry, we'll get her safe no matter what it takes." Paul seemed relieved.

At the nurse's station, a doctor was explaining to Lane. "Yes, medically Amy can release herself today. Her friend Dave can, too. The police don't want them to go home for at least a couple days due to the unknown nature of the threat."

Will shared his first two thoughts with Lane. "My place upstate, or a rental near you? I can rent a house in the name of a trust I have, nobody will trace them there. Get them untraceable phones and they're invisible. I'll arrange nursing and security anywhere they go."

Lane kissed his cheek. "Near me..."

Will pressed the 'Seamus' button on his phone. "Hi, Shay... I need to rent a large furnished house near Sound Beach. Also nursing care available 24/7 and armed security. Run it through that trust... right...okay... you heard about the lawyers shot in Manhattan a while ago? Amy's one of them...no, she'll be fine. I want to get Amy, a couple of her friends and their families out of the city... right...thanks, bud."

He turned back to Lane. "Give him an hour, he'll set the whole thing up. Seamus is really good at this stuff." She relaxed visibly.

When Will and Lane got back in the room, Paul and Amy were kissing rather emphatically. "Ahem... we'll thank you not to excite the patient..." Amy sat back in the chair. "We're making arrangements. You'll go from here to a rental in Sound Beach. Your friends Dave and Charlie can come too. Only you, mom, Paul, Seamus and I will know exactly where you are. You'll have nursing care and security..." he saw the look in Amy's eyes.

"No. I mean, no thank you. I'm not running away. I might take a couple days off, but I'm not really that hurt. I'll be back at work by Friday." She seemed fierce. "Let Dave and Charlie go to a safe house, and take their families too. If this guy can miss from three feet, I'm not worried."

Paul had an idea. "At least stay at my place. Be hard to find if anyone is looking. Spend a week and let NYPD have a chance to find out what's what."

Amy seemed more pleased at this idea. She looked at Lane and Will, who were nodding their heads. "Okay, one week. I'm back next Wednesday." Paul muttered "Maybe" under his breath.

....

Will sent Lane home in his hired car, and took a cab to his own place. He called Seamus again. "Hey, dude... yeah, I'm home... Harvey was all worried... Amy declined my idea, she's going to stay with her detective boyfriend.... Yeah, still rent the house, her friends should duck out of sight, maybe take their families on a vacation... hey, you know a lot of people... know anybody who would have information the police don't? ... yeah... somebody with better connections to our mystery shooter, or news thereof... yeah? See what you can do. Thanks."

One tall bourbon coming up. And explain to Harvey.

After a cloudy afternoon, Thursday dawned clear and bright. Seamus called at 9:00AM to say that Will had a lunch date the next day with somebody with more connections than anybody else Seamus knew. Will kept the appointment.

6

Ciccoli's was a classic Italian restaurant. When Will opened the door, all those good herbs and spices surrounded him, followed by the scent of tomato and roasted meats. He smiled.

"Mister MacLeish, Mister Weiss is in the back dining room. This way, please." Will wondered about the difference in the two names.

A well-dressed man, at least ten years older than Will, stood and extended his hand. "Welcome. I'm Michael Weiss. Mind if I call you Will? Seamus has told me good things about you. Please, have a seat. Would you like something to eat?" Will shook his head. "Not much of an appetite since yesterday."

The two men in the corners of the room didn't move. "I came to ask a favor. Seamus says that you know more people than anybody else he knows, so I'm asking if you can help find the man who shot my daughter and her friends. Maybe you know somebody who heard something?"

Michael was silent a moment. "Well, I heard about the shooting on the news, but nothing more."

"Could I ask you to ask all those people you know? Put the word out, so to speak? I think the police are limited in what they can find out, as a member of the community you might not be."

"Hmmm. I suppose it's true that I know a lot of people, and they in turn know even more. And maybe more can be found out than the police could get. What should happen to this person, this shooter?"

Will took a breath. "They should go to trial. As a mystery writer, I know that some motives for violence should be punished differently than others, and I only want what's reasonable. This person should turn themselves in to the police. My understanding is that it will go easier on them that way."

Michael grinned. "Geez. You're a better man than I am. Somebody shot one of my kids I would want them crucified. I think it's a reasonable thing you're asking for, so yeah. I'll ask around, see what I can come up with. Can I ask a favor from you?"

"Of course. Anything."

"I have a grandson, he's fourteen and wants to be a writer. Name's Giorgio. Could you talk to him, maybe give him some tips on how to succeed at it?"

Will relaxed. "Sure. Has he written anything already?"

"Yeah. Started when he was eight, he writes a story every Christmas, as a present to the family. I'm no critic, but I like his stories; look forward to them. Whaddya say?"

"Sure. Be glad to. Could I get a copy of his latest story, so I know who I'm talking to?"

Michael grinned again. "Just so happens... I brought a copy. If you're free for dinner next Saturday, we're having a big do for my wife's birthday. She loves Romance novels, so I know she'd be crazy to meet you..."

Will took the pages. "Saturday. Here?"

Michael nodded. "Yeah. 8PM. Yes?"

"I'd be glad to. First restaurant I've been in that smells like fresh herbs and fresh tomatoes from the back yard. Love it."

"So maybe now I can talk you into something. Maybe some coffee and a pastry?"

"Sure. That sounds good, actually."

After coffee, Will fell for an invitation to "...a proper lunch..." and didn't leave for two hours. The two men chatted about family, and business, and working hard. They discovered that they had attitudes in common, and shared a love of good food. Along the way, Will had to satisfy his curiosity. "So your name is Weiss, and this is Ciccoli's..."

"Yeah. Great story. This place has been here, pretty much as you see it, for more than sixty years. Three generations of Ciccolis worked here and made it a neighborhood institution. I came here a lot. Then the patriarch decided he wanted to sell, for whatever reason. I told him I'd give more than he was asking, if I got all the recipes and as many of the staff as wanted to work here. Long story short, I bought the whole thing including the manager. He's been here about thirty years, and he's training the next guy for when he retires. The place gets to stay the same, and I get an occasional free meal. I love it."

"That is so cool. So many places get bought out and lose their personality. Glad you could save this one."

As Will left, he mentioned "If this is lunch, I'll have to not eat until next Saturday if I want dinner to fit!" Michael laughed. "You don't eat you'll waste away! Just go light, if anything." Waving, he let the door close. Will felt like he had an ally in this search.

When Will got home, Harvey was asleep on the couch. The dog barely looked up. Will went over to his computer, intent on forcing his story with the interlacing plots to get a few pages toward the finish. He was ready for a struggle, but the plots all started to fall into place. Fifty pages and six hours later, he was forced to take a break. Harvey wanted to go out.

The spring evening struck Will as particularly beautiful, but he hadn't brought the camera. There was still traffic, but not much. One of the things he liked about this neighborhood was that rush hour lasted about forty minutes, from six to six forty five. Here he was at a few minutes after eight, and there were six cars moving. Two of them were headed out for the evening.

In the soft light, Will found himself thinking of Harriet. Charming, articulate, gorgeous... he wondered how long a relationship between them could last. Maybe a long time, if she didn't get tired of his long-time bachelor habits. Maybe he could ask Bob for some tips. As they turned the corner to the church, Harvey started pulling. Will was going to go around to the rectory entrance, but noticed someone sitting on the steps. Harvey ran up, tail wagging, and put his head on the woman's lap.

"Hi, Will."

"Harriet! We were just thinking of you. Mind some company?"

"Not at all. Friendly faces always welcome."

"So what brings you? Doesn't seem like walking distance..."

"No. I came to get some advice from Bob."

"And you got it?"

"Sure, if you consider '...follow your courageous heart, not your overcautious mom mind...' advice."

"Aah, heart troubles?"

"Not exactly. My heart is convinced, and won't let me think of anything else. My brain, that has kept me away from a lot of trouble, says to be careful. To pull back."

Will leaned over and kissed her. Fortunately, Harvey had left a space. When Harriet kissed him back, Will had to fight the impulse to start singing and dancing up and down the steps. "My guess is that Bob is as close to a wise man as I have ever met. Hope that you don't mind me piggy-backing on your advice."

She leaned over and kissed him again. "Is there someplace we could sit that's not made of stone?"

Will led the way to his place. Along the way, she took his hand. "Feels wrong not to hold your hand. Hope you don't mind..."

Will was grinning too much to mind. "Nah... it's nice. I hope it's not jumping the gun here, but since we seem to be going toward something I thought I'd ask, where do you see us going? Only fair to tell you that I will probably leave for a vacation in Scotland in a couple weeks."

Harriet chuckled. She stopped walking and looked him straight in the eyes. "Funny you should ask. I've been thinking about that very thing, and I think I have the perfect answer. Our 20th anniversary is going to be a two-day, four block street fair, with more music, food and games than you've ever seen in one place."

Will listened, then wrapped her in his arms. "Of course, there's that possibility, too. I can see that."

Upon walking through Will's front door, Harriet gasped. "Oh God, you're rich."

Will called out "Security on... new guest." The voice came back "Welcome, Will. Please identify your guest."

"This is Harriet, full guest privileges." He turned to her, whispering. "The security system confirms identity from a silhouette and voice print. If you'd rather not, I can skip it."

Harriet shook her head. In a clear voice she proclaimed "Hello, security, I'm Harriet. Pleased to meet you."

The voice came back. "Welcome, Harriet. Pleased to meet you, too."

It was Will's turn to chuckle. "Poor thing wasn't pleased to meet me, at first. It's gotten a lot better lately. About the place: I got it twenty years ago for when I'm in town. Somebody had to sell immediately. Part of the purchase price was a signed copy of everything I write. Seamus is still sending those first printings every time. I think I paid about a tenth of what it would go for now."

Harriet lounged on the couch. "Still, it's gorgeous and comfortable at the same time."

Will looked at her, and had an idea. "Hey, mind if I take a picture of you? I just got a new camera, and…"

Harriet grinned. "Sure. Anywhere in particular?"

"I've always liked the afternoon light through the big window…"

"Come on, then. Let's take some pictures!"

When Will came back with the camera, Harriet was looking pensively out the window. Click. "Turn toward me a little?" She turned.

"Holy Shit… a Leica?"

"Yeah. A friend of mine made me read a story about a guy that had one for 40 years, really enjoyed it. I got her one for her birthday, thought I'd like one too."

"So you walked into a camera store and bought two of these, probably didn't blink an eye…"

"Well, it was a bunch of money, but it made a friend truly happy. She deserves it. Takes a lot of pictures. How about we try the other side of the window, the light coming in behind you?"

Harriet moved to the other position, leaning against the window frame. "Yeah. Great." Click, adjust the camera, click.

"Hold on, I have an idea that'll make this even better." She stretched out of her top. Nothing under it, and stood smiling at Will.

Will was a little stunned. "You sure?"

"What, do I look unsure? Besides, that machine is great at skin. I've done some modeling. Strictly art, you know. The more skin the better." She lowered her skirt to below her hipbone. "That ought to do it."

Will mustered his composure. Focus. Adjust. Click click click.

Harriet walked over to him. "Let's see how good you are, Mister Photographer. She paged through the shots, and showed him the last one. "See? That made it much better. Nice exposure, nice focus… You should keep that one."

Will looked. "Maybe someplace private." He put down the camera and kissed her with some passion. After about 45 minutes of sincere affections from both of them, the phone rang. "I always answer if I'm here." Harriet pouted, but let him go.

"Hello?... Oh hi, how's things?...Yeah?... Oh. Well, after that drive, he might be ready to talk. Right, I'll be careful. See ya, and thanks." Will came back to the bedroom looking troubled.

"What's up, buttercup?"

"Oh, apparently, a friend is coming after me with a shotgun. His wife just called."

"And here I thought you hadn't done that for a while."

"Oh, I haven't. This couple are good friends from upstate. She's the one I bought the camera for. They live right down the road from me. Apparently, it struck the wrong nerve when he found out how much the camera cost."

"Well yeah, somebody buying the wife almost ten grand worth of anything could make a guy think it's a seduction..."

"You know cameras..."

"Yeah, There's a girl I went to school with does photography. She has a couple different cameras from like the seventies, and a Leica ad framed on her bedroom wall."

"So I wouldn't blame you if you wanted to leave before mister shotgun gets here."

"Oh hell no! Nobody shoots you before I find out how far we can get. As a matter of fact, nobody gets in the door with a shotgun." She picked up the phone. "Describe him."

Will wondered why, but answered. "Five ten, maybe 250, pale skin, light brown hair, probably wearing jeans, jean jacket, plaid flannel shirt."

Harriet dialed. "Hey, James? Would you do me a favor? Somebody's coming after my maybe new boyfriend with a shotgun... yeah... 420 Broome St. ... yeah, right? Guy's white, pale skin, five ten, 250, light hair, probably wearing denim and a flannel shirt. Driving in from Rome... soon as you can, babe... Thank you so much... he's a friend, so just take the gun and let him up. These boys got some talking to do. Thanks again... hey, Jalapeno burgers on me... see you."

Will wondered "So what's up?"

"In about ten minutes, there will be two three hundred pound guys outside the door, waiting to deprive your friend of his weapon, so you can talk."

"Geez... guess I better be nice to you, huh?"

"Nothing more than what we were just doing, I've known James forever, and he'll go a long way to prevent violence. He's known for that in the neighborhood."

Will let the front desk know Morris was coming, and that the two big guys were okay. "Security off." and the light went out. He didn't want to have to explain the system to an agitated Morris.

When Morris got to the door and pounded, he was redfaced with rage, and screaming. "Damnit! City drivers try to kill me all the way down here, then I get frisked by your freakin nig..."

Will's fist impacted Morris' gut in just the right place, with just enough force to knock the wind out of him. Morris sat down against the door.

"You know better, bud. Better than to talk like that around me."

After a minute he was mumbling. "...seduce my wife ya bastard..."

Will understood, mostly, and sat beside him. "Jane's my friend, just like you are. I'm not seducing anybody."

The mumbling continued. "Ten grand... who spends that on somebody's wife without expecting something?"

Will almost laughed. "Me, dude! I told you I had money... and Jane knows that all I would ever expect from her is friendship... a smile when we see one another, a sympathetic ear when I need one.

" That's the way it is, and anything else is just your fears. By the way, you have nothing to worry about. Jane doesn't want anyone or anything but you. You can relax and be a little nicer to her. Smile when you look at her. You can believe anything she says to you."

There was silence for a while, then Morris spoke, sounding normal again. "I get so worried. I can't take it. You're way better looking, and rich..."

Will couldn't resist a chuckle. "Now, Morris... if better looking and more money mattered to Jane, she would have married somebody else. She chose you because of who you are. She stays with you because of who you are now. Now, can we get off the floor and sit like a couple guys? Want a drink?"

"Yeah, then no. I better not drink if I'm gonna turn around and go home."

"So don't. Stay over. But first, call Jane and apologize for making her worry. Tell her I need somebody to sit around drinking with. And by the way, where's the shotgun?"

"What?"

"Jane called, said you left with a shotgun."

Morris' turn to chuckle. "Man, I left that off to get adjusted. Damn thing's old, ya have to let a professional at them sometimes."

Harriet came out of the bedroom. "Seems like the start of a guys' night out. I think I'll just fade back whence I came." She kissed Will on the cheek. "I look forward to meeting you in better circumstances, Morris." She stopped at the door. "Sunday?"

Will's natural, quiet smile appeared. "Absolutely." He hadn't noticed the stunned look on Morris' face yet. His smile grew. "New romance. I think it might go somewhere. The guys at the door were friends of hers, being protective."

Morris took a couple beats to let that sink in. "Holy moly, Batman... been a while for you, too."

"Yeah, years. A local minister thought we should meet, and apparently he was right. Hey, I bet you haven't eaten yet."

"Leftover sausages, potatoes and biscuits, about five."

Will shook his head. "Let me show you a proper city lunch. There's a place right down the street. We can spend a couple hours drinking, too."

Morris stood up. His opinion of city food was that one had a choice between lots of grease and salt or a carrot carved into a rose. He did, however know that Will wouldn't settle for anything not good enough to compete with Jane's leftovers. He would give Will a chance.

Once they got through their large plates covered with half pound lean burgers, Blue cheese fries and onion rings you could use as bracelets, Morris admitted to himself that he should always trust Will about food. To Will, he expressed all that with a "Hmmmmmmm."

Then the beer started coming. Will ordered a rotation, in which each round of beer was a different brew. "So Morris... you don't think Jane is interested in you?"

"Aah, not exactly that... I figure I'm not as fascinating as most guys. After all, I'm just a farmer. That's what I spend my time thinking and worrying about. If the crops fail, I don't know what to do."

"Yeah. Survival is important, and for your survival to depend on this one thing..."

"That's never going to pay enough to save anything for old age..."

Will nodded. "You know what I've heard makes people interesting?"

"What?"

"Being interested in something else. Something not about survival."

"What?"

"I mean, like Larry Houlihan. He spends some time carving wood. People love those little figures he does."

"Yeah, I got a couple. He's real good."

"Well, the time he spends carving is time he's not worrying about his farm. Plus, it gives him something else to talk about. Here's a thought (yes, we'll have another round)... when you were a kid, what did you want to be when you grew up?"

Morris looked at him like that was the single most useless question in the world. "Why?"

"Maybe you could do something besides farming once in a while, be more interesting."

"Oh. Okay, when I was a kid. What did I want? I wanted to be a singer, like Bing Crosby. Every time there was some music on TV, I wanted to be a singer. Wanted to be an Irish Tenor."

Will was taken aback. "A singer. So why have I never heard you sing?"

"Aah, it's just a dream..."

"Can you sing?"

"Used to, in church."

Will scratched his head. "I want to hear this. There's a karaoke machine in the back room that I bet we could use." To the bartender "Hey John, can we use the karaoke for a bit?" The bartender gave the thumbs up. "C'mon, Mo...You sing one I'll sing one."

Among the selection of available genre CDs, Will found Oldies. On a guess, he thought that both he and Morris would be familiar with them. He fired up the machine and turned on the lights. "Okay, mister 'I'm just a farmer', lets see what else you are." He handed Morris the microphone.

Morris had had just enough beer to humor his neighbor. He took the mike and looked through the selections. "Oh… I like this one." He pressed the button. The stage light prevented him from seeing Will start to record with his cell phone. The song was 'Pretty Woman'. Morris was about halfway through when Will saw John standing in the doorway, listening.

"He's way better than you are, and you're not so bad." Morris finished, and applause came through from the other room.

"That one always makes me think of Jane."

Will was impressed. "Holy wowzir! Where have you been hiding THAT?"

Morris, suddenly embarrassed. "I got one of those little music things, throw it in my pocket and the buds in my ears, especially when I'm plowing or something. Sounds better than the tractor engine. I sing along."

"Dude! You should share this with people. Doesn't the bar back in town do a karaoke night?"

"Sure. Wednesdays."

"You should definitely go!"

A few people wandered in from the bar. "Is there going to be more singing?"

Will pointed at Morris. "You'll have to ask the singer."

Morris decided that if people wanted him to, he would oblige. More beer arrived, on Will's calculation that it would keep him buzzed enough to perform, but not so much to interfere with the performance.

Half an hour later, Morris took a break. "Wow, Will… I never would have thought of that. That was fun."

Will put his hand on the singer's shoulder. "I'm sorry to have to tell you this, but you'll never be an Irish tenor. You're a baritone, like that nice Crosby fella." Both of them laughed. "By the way, that first song is going on YouTube. The world should know."

"Aah, you're nuts."

"Maybe. Want to do some more, or get back to my place?"

"Back, I suppose. These folks have put up with enough."

Seeing him walk out, the audience moaned their disappointment. John stepped up. "Your bill is paid if you do two more songs. This one and this one." Not being the type to refuse a free meal, Morris agreed.

After Morris' versions of "Accentuate the Positive" and "White Christmas", the room was silent. People who had never heard the first, and only seen the movie of the second were lost in a dream. When he tried to leave, the small crowd stood. John asked for all of them "Where can we get your records?"

Morris was stunned. "There aren't any. Really, I'm just a farmer from upstate!"

Will consoled them. "I got the whole thing on my phone. Watch YouTube for Morris Jamison." The audience erupted in cheers, and let the two men leave. Back at Will's, they sat for a while.

"Wow. I came down here ready to fight you for my wife, now I want to hug you. Guess I'm feeling a little windblown. Don't do anything with the video for at least a week, wouldja?"

"Sure. Even if you want me to erase them. Anything you want."

At 8:00 that night, Morris had another coffee after two servings of Will's spaghetti when he fell asleep with his hand on the cup.

Early the next morning, Will and Morris worked their way through Will's version of a farm breakfast. During coffee afterward, the buzzer sounded for the front door. Will wondered if the doorman was on a break. "Hello?"

The voice came back, a little shaky. "Hey, it's Amy. Can I come up?"

"Of course!" He pushed to unlock the door. Morris thought to leave. "No need. Stick around, finish your dessert and coffee, relax a little. I do wonder what's up, she sounded nervous."

Amy got through the door and gave Will a big hug, holding on a little long. "Hey there... what's the matter? Here, sit. Tell me."

"It may just be me going nuts from not going to work, sitting around Paul's place, but maybe I don't want to be a lawyer any more. I definitely don't want to get shot for doing my job ever again."

Will held her hand. "Sure. I get that. Any possibility of another firm? Getting away from criminal law?"

"I suppose. I just realized that the last year and a half has been twelve and fourteen hour days, six days a week. Maybe that's too much. I do want to have a life some day. Here I thought Lawyer was the ultimate office job, but I got shot. And it could have been a lot worse. How can I go back there?"

Will thought about that a minute. "I have to admit, I worry about you. It's rare for lawyers to be shot at, but it happens. With this investigation into corruption in the city government you could run into some really bad people, and that case could last a year or more."

Morris had been quietly listening. "Will, why don't you ask her the question you asked me?"

Amy suddenly noticed that there was someone else in the room. "Oh...you've got a guest... hope I'm not intruding..."

"Not at all. This is Morris, my neighbor from upstate. He just needed to get out of the house for a while, he's on his way back in the morning."

Morris filled her in. "Will solved a problem I didn't even know was a problem. He asked me one question. We had lunch and a few beers, so I answered the question and it led somewhere. Now I got at least a new hobby. I'm a farmer, so I can relate to the long hours doing your job. The question might help."

Amy looked at Will and shrugged. "So ask..."

Will stood up and poured Amy a short drink. "I know it's a little early, but drink this, and I'll ask." Amy drained the glass, and Will asked. "When you were young, what was your fantasy of what you would do when you grew up? Who did you want to be?"

Amy closed her eyes. "Jessica Fletcher. You know, from 'Murder, She Wrote'. Mom and I loved that show. She got to travel, and write, had friends and relatives... that seemed like the life."

Will tried unsuccessfully to hide a grin. "A lot of lawyers have found fame and fortune as writers, maybe you could too. Plus, I know an agent."

Amy shook her head. "Maybe not... writing is a solitary activity."

"Yes, but done right it can leave lots of time for a life. And I could be your guide. At first, I spent about 60 hours a week planning and writing. Now, I plan in my head, and it takes up to a month full-time to write a novel. Less for essays. That's how I get away with three books a year. The rest of the time I'm being a neighbor, friend, and citizen."

"Really?"

"Sure. I'd be excited to have you join the family business. You have a few days off, give it a try. Start with a short story. Ten or fifteen pages might not be so hard..."

Amy squinted at him. "Seducing me away from my career?"

"Providing an alternative. Maybe you wind up doing both, or neither. Childhood dreams are important."

"So what was yours?"

Morris chimed in. "Yeah, Will, what was yours? Turnabout's fair play..."

"Okay, okay... first, I wanted to be Ansel Addams. Then I wanted to be Isaac Asimov. By the time I was ten, my folks had gotten me a camera and a typewriter. Through school, I considered Journalism."

Amy's turn to chuckle. "Then you took that abrupt turn into left field."

"Yeah. At least, I got into writing pretty easily. And now I've got a camera again. Maybe my dreams are coming true after all."

Amy hugged him. "You're a little nuts, but I love you. And I will give it a try, your short story idea. Maybe it's nothing, but maybe it's something. At least I won't be sitting around wondering where the next shot is coming from."

Morris felt the need to embarrass Will a little. "By the way, have you heard about the new girlfriend?"

Will sighed. "Really?"

Amy was fascinated. "New girlfriend? What's she like?"

Morris was eager to gossip. "Gorgeous, gracious, and protective. Great smile. Oh hey, look at the time. I will drive back now. Nobody on the highway, and I bet my wife will want to talk to me. Nice meeting you Amy... Will, I'll let you know." Morris flew out the door.

Amy was still on the subject. "So what's her name?"

Will put his arm around her. "Harriet. We met through a mutual friend. She has two sons, and so far we spent an afternoon at a church fair, had dinner out with the boys, and spent some time here. She was here when Morris arrived yesterday. When he saw her he went all teenager about it. He knows I don't date much."

Amy hugged him. "Well good for you. I can't wait 'til mom hears about this."

"Hey, hey... no need to bother your mom with my possible love life. I kinda just met her. Let's see where it goes before we make a news article out of it."

When Amy left, more calmly than she had arrived, Will found himself alone with a far too complex plot. He took a nap.

7

Saturday arrived, as Saturdays will, and Will was ready. For an April birthday, a tan suit with a pale gray shirt and tan tie with gold threads woven through it. He picked up a small box with gift card, and headed out.

The taxi pulled up to the restaurant at five minutes of eight, and Weiss met him at the door. "I knew it! Right on time. Hi, Will… dinner's a little delayed, and I got some news. Let's sit a minute." The two men slid into a booth.

"News is, we found your shooter." Weiss looked at his watch. "He's turning himself in right about now. Turns out, he's a decent enough guy… never even got a speeding ticket. He was running a scam on the city, and somebody gave that law firm a bunch of ideas where to look, what people might be doing. He's got a second cousin works for the firm.

"So anyway, the cousin tells him to cover his tracks and get out of the scam, he can't figure out how, and goes nuts. This is a third of his income, after all. With prices rising faster than salaries, he had to do something.

"I talked to the guy. Guaranteed him his family would be okay, and he'd have a job when he got out, if he did the right thing. Got him a lawyer who says he might only do ten years on six counts and the scam. He was relieved about that. So you can tell your daughter it was just a one-off, and she's pretty safe otherwise."

Will relaxed a bit. "Wow. That's in just a few days. Thank you, Michael. That's fantastic."

Weiss continued. "There's time before dinner yet. Seamus is in the bar, I'll let him tell you the even weirder thing that came up when I asked about you getting attacked in the park. We're in the back room when you're done."

Will shook his hand and headed to the bar. "Hey, Shea, What's up?"

Seamus sat at a table, looking like a man with troubles. "Hey, Will. I'm so sorry..."

"About what?"

"Weiss found out who attacked you, and why. It was some teenagers, hired to scare you. My bookie hired them. I owe about a quarter million, and he wanted the money faster than I could pay. He thought the insurance money would cover it. There's a half million dollar policy in that new contract you signed. I'm so sorry, Will. I never figured him for that bad a guy.

"Weiss turned him in, and he got arrested yesterday, on criminal conspiracy to commit murder. The black car on the sidewalk was his nephew. Fortunately, the kid wasn't up for actually killing somebody. I'm so sorry."

Will put a hand on his shoulder. "How could you know? People are nuts. Do you still owe all that?"

Seamus mumbled "Yeah."

"Let me cut you a check, make it go away. We'll figure it was an investment that went sour. But no more bookies, okay?"

"Oh Jesus, Will. You don't have to... I mean..."

"Look, I won't have my agent and my editor distracted with this debt hanging over. You've got work to do. Now go home and sleep it off. Then spend some time with your family. We can have lunch, Wednesday maybe. You won't believe this new book I'm working on. It'll need your full attention." Will half-hugged him, stood up and headed toward the party in the back room, shaking his head over Seamus. That's too much gambling debt to get into before asking your best friend for help.

The party was attended by about two dozen people, arranged at one long table. As soon as Will walked in, a woman turned and recognized him instantly.

"William MacLeish! Oh my God!"

Michael Weiss stood. "Darling, this is our new friend Will. I thought you would like to meet a favorite author. Will, my rather excited wife, Cassandra."

The woman grabbed Will. "Here, sit by me."

Will reached into his pocket for a small box. Too big for a ring, too small for a necklace. "Happy birthday. Thought you might enjoy this."

When she opened the box, her eyes went wide, and her jaw relaxed. "Ooh... roses! I love roses. And they're made of glass?"

Will provided background. "Yes, they are. A little gift shop near me carries them. I am assured that they are not too fragile, despite how delicate they seem. And this one can be a pin or a necklace. See, there's a mounting on the back."

Cassandra was amazed. "I've never seen anything like this. It's amazing. Thank you so much!" She hugged him until Michael's smile at her happiness started to fade. "And now, the first course!"

Between courses, there were a few minutes when people could stand, and go talk to those at the other end of the table. Before the entrée, a large break was announced: Ten minutes. Will looked for the fourteen year old boy.

"Hi, Giorgio?"

"Yes sir. Are you really a famous author?"

"Aah, maybe successful is a better word. I support myself, and my agent makes some too. I understand that you like to write…"

"Oh sure. I do a story at Christmas, as a gift to the family. Not having money to buy something, it seemed like an option."

Will smiled. "I used to make fancy hand decorated Christmas cards when I didn't have money for gifts. I think you made the right choice to do stories, though. Your grandfather showed me one…"

"Oh gosh, sorry about that."

"No, I'm glad he did. I think it's really good. You have a good sense of story, and a way with words. And you write impressively well. Are you thinking of a career in fiction?"

"Well sure, I'd love that… but I would also like to do some journalism, some history…"

"I can see that happening for you. What do they have you reading in school these days?"

"Oh, ummm… Nathaniel Hawthorne, Poe, and Aeschylus."

"Wow. That's some variety. You keep up with all that?"

"Sure. Have to. But I would like to read something more current, like the last ten years or so."

Will reached into his pocket. "Then I've got the perfect thing for you. A list of the best short story writers in the world, all of whom are alive, so you can write to them. My contact info is there, too, in case you need any advice.

"Thinking of advice, I brought some of that, too. You should consider not getting a Creative Writing degree. You have that part down pat, and I think you'll get better the more you write. Remember, Hawthorne, Poe and Aeschylus got by without one. Study things you're interested in, and write about them. That'll make you happier, and a better writer."

"Wow. I hadn't thought of it that way. Thanks, Mr. MacLeish. And thank you for those nice things you said about my writing. I really appreciate it."

Michael caught up with Will as he walked away. "Thanks for that. I haven't seen him smile that big since he was little."

"To tell the truth, it's a good thing I'm winding down the writing. I don't want to compete with him. I do okay, but he could be important."

Then there was lamb. The scent of delicately seasoned meat wandered through the kitchen doors and planted itself in Will's nostrils, making him salivate.

It was a little before 11:00 PM when the family let him leave. He made the excuse of not wanting to fall asleep in the cab. Mike and Cassandra reminded him not to be a stranger. When he finally opened his own door, Amy was curled up on the couch. Harvey was on the floor beside her, on guard. Will got a little wag of the tail for coming home.

"Oh, Will... I didn't know where else to go. I was in the apartment, dinner ready. Paul got home in a rage. Broke off the key in the lock, he was screaming. He got inside and all he could do was rant, something about work... he got madder and madder, finally punched a hole in the wall. Then he looked at me. I grabbed my purse and ran, scared as I've ever been. It was like Dr. Jekyll and Mr. Hyde. I'm still scared if he comes here."

Will wrapped his arms around her. "He's not going to get in." He stroked her hair. "Security System..."

"Yes, Will?"

"Paul DeVries, Change to no entry."

"Clearance changed."

They sat there for a while, quiet. Then Amy spoke again. "Why me? This is why I'm not with somebody. Nobody I meet is actually even stable."

Will thought it might be a little soon, but asked anyway. "Mind if I find out if he's still in one piece? Trying to beat up a wall, a guy could get hurt."

Amy looked at him, surprised. "Okay. Don't want him hurt."

Will took out his phone and poured himself a Bourbon. "Hey, Paul? You okay?... Yeah, I heard. What happened?...(long pause)... Oh Jeesh. I can see how that would hurt... You did?... Well yeah... then you got home... yeah, you did... you are? Good... I will... give it the two months anyway, find out about the rest of that, then we'll see. Take care of yourself, man... get to a doctor... I'll stay in touch."

He turned back to Amy. "Six months of investigation, the FBI takes over, suspect turns state's evidence. He punched an Assistant District Attorney, and took a swing at his Captain. Suspended for two months, pending a Psych review. He figures his career is over, and now it's over with you. He's quiet now, but I told him to work out what he had to, give it that couple months before contacting you. One thing at a time."

"What was that about a doctor?"

"All that punching, his hand was swelling. Might be broken."

"Oh."

"Hey, want a drink?"

"Had one when I got in."

"Want another? This qualifies as a big deal."

"No, maybe just a blanket." Will went to get one.

"Oh, I have news about the shooting." That perked her up. "The shooter turned himself in tonight. Just one guy, went nuts. No conspiracy."

"Oh. Good." Her eyes closed for the night. Will kissed her forehead. As he lay down to sleep, there was a thought. He picked up the phone. "Hi, Lane, it's Will. I figured your mom reflexes would be tingling... yeah... a little tension earlier. She's here now, got out of the tense situation like a pro... Oh, and they found the shooter. Turned himself in... not a criminal, except for this one incident... just snapped... right... so at least that's over, except for the echoes of worry, when something comes out of nowhere like that... Sure, you're welcome. Good night."

In the morning over bagels, Amy seemed better, but contemplative. "I wish I could get the relationship that this one seemed to be going toward. Wish I could find the right guy, so mom would have to find something else to bug me about."

"Like having kids?"

Amy shook her head. "Or anything else in the world…"

Will smiled. "Right. I guess I've been lucky, she doesn't know what to bug me about."

"Hmph. Lucky indeed. Of course, there's the new girlfriend…"

Will was silent for a moment.

"Nerve?"

"Nah, well maybe. I've been thinking I want to be back upstate. Big city might not be my native habitat. I've spent twenty some years up there, the happy hermit. New girlfriend would imply that I was staying here."

Amy nodded. "Yeah, the city's losing a little luster for me too. Last night I woke up thinking that I could move back near mom, probably get work doing something people don't get shot for."

"Sure. Your mom and I would appreciate your avoidance of that kind of event." Harvey leaned his head on Will's lap. "And Harvey, too. I always get the idea that he knows everything. That he wishes he had been there to protect you. I know he seems like a cuddlebunny, but there were coyotes up by the cabin a couple years ago, and I swear he chased them off. His voice can be quite impressive." Harvey spun around wagging his tail like a propeller. Will gave him a little piece of bagel with lox, which disappeared in a flash, and engendered a puppy-eyed plea for more.

Will had a thought. "Hey, could you do with some church this morning?"

Amy hadn't thought of it. "Church?"

"Yeah. I'm feeling quite thankful this morning. We're both here, and well. I figure sometimes that requires some more formal recognition. I met the pastor, seems nice."

"Sure, I get the gratitude thing. I keep thinking… a couple inches left, I wouldn't be here. Sure, let's go. Don't know if I'm dressed for it."

"No worries. I get the impression it's 'Come as you are'."

"Okay then. When is it?"

"Ten. We have time for more bagel."

When they arrived, at 9:50, the pews were about half full. The service started exactly on time, when Will realized that he didn't know what denomination the place was. He supposed that it wouldn't matter. Introductory prayers, worshipful prayers, then thankful ones. Will appreciated that they sounded familiar.

Then Bob came to face the congregation. Will guessed that this would be the sermon.

"Ladies and gentlemen, friends and visitors, today I would like to speak about something besides the readings. Two subjects that I haven't heard in a church before, but that I think deserve your attention as conscientious members of this community.

"The first is fear. A good friend recently sent me an editorial essay from a small newspaper. The article pointed out very well the similarity between fear and a highly communicable disease. Sometimes, a disease can sit in the human body, affecting functions one doesn't notice. Fear is like that, an undertow changing mental processes before you notice. One can become more and more cautious, and put it down to experience. One can venture outside their comfort zone less and less, and rationalize that those things outside the border aren't necessary.

"As Christians, we have cause not to fear. 'As I walk through the Valley of Death I shall fear no evil for thou art with me…' is the ultimate proclamation against fear. After all, if I don't fear death, what of the billions of smaller things in life should I fear? None.

"I urge you today to examine your lives for evidence of fear. For things you haven't done, or have done because of social conventions, because it's in your job definition or you think it is. Things you think you're too old for, too dignified for. Things you've always heard you're no good at, but could give you joy.

"Folks, fear keeps people away from love, therefore away from God, since God is Love. Love is what disassembles fear. I urge you to look for what fear urges you toward or away from, and defy that urging with all the force you can muster.

"As an example, I have wanted for some time to get a bicycle, to ride for fun and exercise. What has kept me from that joy is fear that it is below the dignity of my position as pastor. Recently, however, I thought that what is beneath the dignity of my position is to become out of shape, and less than energetic in my guidance of all you good people toward God.

"With the thought that a shepherd that can't walk, or chase off wolves, is not a good shepherd, I am going to get a bicycle, and you might see me wheeling around the neighborhood. You might even, some day, see me on a long charity ride. I don't know. But as I age, as we all must, I will not be sedate in my work, for what I have chosen to do is more important than my comfort.

"And that brings me to my second subject: Right Work. I have come across the phrase again as a Buddhist concept, along with Right Thought. Each of us is created with abilities and talents. One of the things we should do in this world is use our talents. Using those talents fulfills part of God's plan, and should thus be encouraged.

"Right Work, ladies and gentlemen, is never boring. It is never a chore. It is never difficult to wake up and do your Right Work, because it's what you were sent here for. Your Right Work, as I understand it, need not be your profession; it just needs to be something you do. Something you do on purpose, that gives your days more meaning than earning money ever can.

"Apparently, friends, I have found my Right Work. I ask you to find yours, and do it. The world needs what you were sent here to do. The world needs desperately the contributions of all of us.

"That makes my monologue complete, leaving you with two things to think about: fight Fear and find your Right Work. I am convinced that these two are God's work in the world. That if we pursue them, the world becomes closer to the place it could be.

"On this beautiful Spring day, I won't take up any more of your time. Those who wish to receive Communion please come up, then we'll say a prayer of thanks and the service will be ended."

A line formed, and the Sacrament performed. When all had been served, Bob stepped forward again. "Go in peace to love and serve in the name of The Lord. I thank you for your attention and I thank God for everything else." Will noticed people dropping contributions in a wicker basket on the way out.

Will and Amy stayed seated as the congregation left. Amy spoke first. "Wow. That's not as I remember. Real advice, as opposed to an explanation? Genius."

Bob's voice came from behind them. "Thanks. I like to shake things up once in a while, keep the service from being the same thing every week. Will, who's your charming companion today?"

Will smiled. "This is Amy, a friend's daughter."

"Glad to meet you, Amy... you're welcome here any time, with or without this dog-owner of a man.

"Actually, Will, I'm glad you're here. I remember you saying something about baking. Do you still do that?"

"Sure, sometimes."

"One of our parishioners is celebrating her hundredth birthday soon, and she expressed a fond memory for something she called 'Orange Cake'. I'm trying to track down a recipe. Have you ever heard of it?"

Will scratched his head. "No, never heard of it. But hearing the words my brain went into high gear thinking how to make one."

"Apparently, she lived in Florida as a girl, and her mother made this cake. Not too sweet, a rich orange taste, and quite fluffy. Her mother put a dusting of something she called 'Lemon Sugar' instead of frosting on top. Any chance you could develop a recipe and make enough for a hundred people by two weeks from yesterday?"

Will chuckled. "I'll need some more clues."

"The only other thing she said was that they didn't have much money, and her mother would go into the kitchen with a box of oranges and come out with the cake. What do you think?"

"Let's see... real oranges, not too sweet, Lemon Sugar. I have an idea what the Lemon Sugar is... give me a couple days. I'll come up with a sample cake, and you can tell me what you think."

"Aw gee, Will... thanks. None of the other bakers had the slightest idea."

"Sure, Bob. I'll let you know." He stood to go.

Amy asked "Do you need a hand cleaning up or anything? I'd like to support any church that follows through on the Enlightenment."

"Sure. Volunteers always welcome."

Amy turned to Will. "You go ahead. I'll be along presently." Then she went off with Bob. Will dropped a hundred in the basket. He considered that his gratitude had been expressed.

Once sitting again on his own couch, Will considered the choice he had to make: pursue a possibly very rewarding relationship and stay in town, or go back up to the cottage and work on a book for four months. He was more comfortable working on the book. He knew how to do that. But Bob's sermon had hit home: don't not do or not do good things out of fear. And Harriet was, he believed, a good thing.

This was going to require a second brain; one unencumbered by his perspective. How about Lane? Always smart and reasonable, except that one day. He could call. As he reached for the phone, it rang. "Hello?...Oh, Lane. I was just reaching for the phone to call you... I need some advice from someone more emotionally mature than I am... What do you mean, you're not... sure, you could come tomorrow, or tonight if need be... Amy's staying with me for a couple days, but we can figure something out if you want to stay over... of course... hey, I didn't hear it at first, but you sound troubled. Hope I can help... yeah, I'll meet your train at Penn Station, 10:00... see you then."

Will knew very well that Lane wasn't the type to take off work for no reason, and now that she said that she had taken the week off, he was worried. Harvey sensed an opening for a hug, and lay on the couch with his front paws stretched across his human's lap.

"I don't know, Harv... everybody seems to think I can solve things. I hope they're right. Oh, you're going to meet Lane, Amy's mother. You'll be on your best behavior, right? And you're probably going to want to follow her home, but don't, okay?"

Harvey sat up straight, a model of his breed, whatever that was. One vet had guessed Akita-Collie-Komondor. There had been no guess as to temperament, but a warning that this would probably be among the smartest canines Will could meet. So far, Harvey had seemed wise and gentle.

When Amy got back, Will was on his third glass of wine. Amy looked at him quizzically. "What is it about you? I meet you, and the detective is worth dating. I go to church with you, and the pastor is even more so. We waltzed, Will. Waltzed. Do you know how rare that is? In the middle of the last room to dust, all the other volunteers had gone, and 'New York State of Mind' comes on the radio. THE LONG VERSION. And we waltzed. Forget the Macarena, the Bump, Grinding... Waltz is a total seduction. When the music ended, he kissed me, so gently and for so long that I would have moved in right then. Jeez, my heart is still fast. What have you done? Are you the leader of a karmic troop of hot guys? Or are you just one of them?"

She stopped talking and sat on the floor, facing him across the coffee table. "Do you have any sedatives? I really should calm down."

Will shook his head. "Nothing pharmaceutical, but I do have a nice herbal tea, all ready for some ice and a tall glass. Care to join me?"

Amy nodded enthusiastically. "Oh... oh no... wine. Am I the most fickle thing on the planet? Turn my back on one relationship I thought was good, and less than 24 hours later want to start another one? Aagh. Maybe this is what I get for not going steady with anybody in high school, or for putting my career first. Aagh."

Will understood. "No, you're not fickle. You have to deal with things as they come up. Paul's going to need a couple months, so there's no harm in not being alone meanwhile. Then you can judge one relationship against the other, with a new knowledge about what Paul is dealing with."

"So you're saying let Bob be a possibility."

"Sure, why not? Being single is a time to check out possibilities, without making a commitment. As long as everyone understands that, everything's good."

"Damn. Wise, too."

"Oh, by the way your mom's coming tomorrow. Said she wanted to get out of the house, talk to somebody with a fresh perspective. I'm meeting her train at 10:00."

"Hmmm... that's new. Want I should disappear?"

"Nah. I can get a futon if she wants to stay. Gosh, if you've met more guys since we met, I've never had so many visitors before." He clinked his glass against hers. "To us! May this all turn out magically, beautifully magnificent."

....

When Lane appeared through the gate, she was walking slowly, and a little hunched over. Seeing Will, she straightened up. "Hi, guy... lookin good."

He wrapped his arms around her. "Even I can tell that something's wrong. Let's sit somewhere and you can tell me." He guided her over to a bench in the waiting room. "Yeah. You could say something's wrong. My husband of the last thirty years, and he's been a fine husband, wants a divorce." She took a beat to let that sink in. "You know, to be fair, when we got married we had a deal. As long as any kids were at least fifteen, either of us could ask for a divorce and the other wouldn't contest it. And hey, he's being more than generous, giving me the house and half the investments. He found someone he needs to be with. That's the other part of our agreement... honesty."

Will took her hand in his. "I don't get how people do stuff like that. How some people can just throw away a thirty year relationship, let alone a marriage."

Lane continued. "He's not coming back. He's going to live the rest of his life in China. I knew he always wanted to go there, like as a tourist... guess it was something more. I just had to get out of the house."

"Yeah. I'm glad you called. Glad to have you around, no matter the circumstances. You going to tell Amy?"

"Sure. I mean, I should. Andy said he'd talk to Patrick, I guess I get to tell Amy. I guess the two of them are old enough not to take it personally, but Amy and Andy... hey, I never realized... wasn't there a comedy duo?"

"Wow. Long time ago. Vaudeville. Amos and Andy."

"Yeah, that's it. Anyway, those two complete one another's sentences. Like they're one mind. It's going to be hard on her."

Will grinned his pixie grin. "Maybe there's something that can soften the blow."

"Like what?"

"She just met my neighborhood pastor yesterday. She likes him."

Lane seemed surprised. "What? What about Paul?"

"There was a major bump in the road on that one. Probably be a couple months before they even talk."

"Oh god, that girl has the worst... a pastor, you say?"

"That's right. Handsome, intelligent, a little wise, even. We went to church yesterday, and Amy stayed a while to help clean. They waltzed, and he kissed her."

"And he can dance?"

"Yeah. Meanwhile, your daughter is trying to figure out if she wants to be a lawyer any more. I told her she has my support no matter what she decides."

"I thought the shooting would engender some introspection. Be interesting to see what she comes up with."

Will remembered the car and driver waiting outside. "Ready to go?"

"Sure. Can't wait to see this bachelor pad in Soho..."

"Hah. Hardly a bachelor pad with my daughter and her mom in it."

Walking into Will's place, Lane was surprised by the amount of light. "Holy cow, Will... it's brilliant in here. Feels like you."

The security system did its job. "Welcome, Will. Please identify your guest. Voice print sufficient." Lane looked around, wide-eyed.

"This is Lane, Amy's mother. Clearance level guest."

"Welcome, Lane... please make yourself comfortable."

Will filled her in. "The security system identifies you by silhouette and voice print. Say something like 'Hi it's me'". Lane obliged with "Hi it's me, I'm here!" and the machine welcomed her.

Amy and Harvey wandered out of the bedroom. "Hey, mom. Oh, what's wrong... could only be that dad's not coming back from China. You okay?"

Lane plopped down on the couch. "How..."

Amy sat beside her and provided a big hug. "I suspected probably before he did. You know how Chinacentric he is... art, history, culture... I would have put even money on whether he came back. Really, are you okay with it?"

Lane shook her head. "I don't know yet. He called yesterday and said he wants a divorce. Met someone, couldn't just have an affair like other people."

"Yeah. The man you married isn't like other men. You know he still loves you, and always will."

"I guess." By this time, Harvey's head was on Lane's lap. "Oh, what a wonderful dog. Harvey, right?" Harvey stood tall and wagged his tail like he was trying to clear off the coffee table.

Will offered an alternative to more emotional conversation. "Anybody for food? We can take out or cook in."

Lane was staring at a print on the wall. "Will... what's this?"

Amy was proud. "Oh yeah. Not only is he a great writer, but he can draw!"

Lane walked up to the image, almost touching it. "Apparently from memory. This is the end of our day together, isn't it?"

For once, Will blushed. "Only you would spot it. Most people think it's an abstract."

"You sentimental old codger, you. That's amazing. And yes, something to eat would be good. Have anything to drink?"

As the good host, Will offered alternatives. "Juices, water, or a tall Bitter Morning?"

"Egad, you remember."

"Of course."

"I'll take one of those." Amy looked quizzical. "Oh honey... you should try one. Will invented this for Sunday brunch. Brought a half gallon pitcher to the Cafeteria. That made all those hangovers disappear, and great conversation took over."

"What's in it?"

"Bitter Lemon and a splash of dark rum. It's delish."

"Okay, maybe a small one. I'm going over to help Bob with a sermon later."

Will and Lane glanced at one another and nodded knowingly. Amy protested. "No, not like that... he just wants some help with the phrasing."

Lane joked "Phrasing. Never heard it called that."

"MOM..."

Lane went back to food and drink. "One and a third Bitter Morning and two Blue Cheese omelets, please." Will went to work.

After brunch, everyone wondered where they had stuffed so much food. Will had added sausages, home fries and herbed biscuits to the simple omelet request. After a little siesta, Lane asked another favor. "Will, could you give us, like an hour? Girl talk, you know..."

Will stood. "C'mon, Harvey... long walk." Harvey considered staying with Lane and Amy, but ambled over to Will with a wistful glance back at Lane.

"Don't worry... we'll be here when you get back." Lane assured him.

Out the front door, Will asked "Which way, dude?" Harvey pulled right, toward the church. "Good idea. We can ask Bob what to do."

Conveniently, Bob was enjoying the front steps again. "Hey, guys..."

"Hey, Bob. I need guidance."

"Okay... what about?"

"Well, Amy's mom is at my place. Her husband asked for a divorce. I can imagine her asking me to come live with her. She's talking about how it's not good to be rambling around the big house when it's just her, and how it has already been lonely."

"Oh. And how is Harriet these days?"

"She's ... wow... Harriet is amazing. Full of energy and life... smart as people get. I'd really like to spend enough time to get to know her."

"So what do you see happening, problem-wise?"

"These two women want me for themselves, and I don't know how to choose."

"Oh, that. Amy's mom was a friend in college, right?"

"Yeah. We spent a bunch of time together as friends for about three years. Really close friends. Then there's that one day. If I had stuck around, we might still be together."

"And where's Amy in all this?"

"I get the feeling she would like to live around here. She sees a possible relationship with you. By the way, what are your intentions?"

Bob took a breath. "Honestly, I can imagine getting very serious very fast. But I don't want her to be running from one relationship to another. Don't want to be a rebound guy."

Will paused. "Right. I told her to deal with things as they come up. She told you about her detective, right?"

"Briefly."

"Between that and the shooting, she might be spooked."

"Right. Well, all I can think to do is spend some time with her, and be careful."

"Yeah. So what about my potential dilemma?"

"I know you wanted to slow down on the writing. What else did you want?"

"Hmmm... a calm life with somebody pleasant... a little writing, a little artwork, some friends. Three books a year doesn't leave a lot of time for anything else. I guess what I was thinking of is a change from so much work. Knowing a few farmers upstate, I see that it takes up all their energy and I didn't want writing to do that to me any more. I guess what I was looking for is the classic small-town life."

"Do you see either of these women fitting in to that picture?"

"Don't know. And don't know if it matters. The picture could change a hundred and eighty degrees. Like it seemed to when I found out Amy was my daughter. More information changes everything."

"Yes, it does. I'd still put a lot of weight on that original picture, though. It's something you wanted when you were just thinking about yourself. Might be what you really want."

"Yeah, guess so." Harvey tired of all this chatter, and pulled toward his long walk. "Gotta go. See ya."

"Bye, Will... Bye Harvey!"

....

So, if Bob was right, the point was to get to that original dream. The one from a couple months ago. The one in which he could be a gracious host occasionally. The one in which he felt that he was, finally, exactly where he belonged. The question right before that seemed to be "How?". Will remembered that he had gotten a passport some months ago. He called Seamus.

"Hey, did I leave my passport in your office?... right... I figure I've never travelled, and travel broadens the mind, so I thought I would do that this summer... Really? Great. I'll roll over tomorrow and pick it up... Thanks, Seamus, for everything... no, I haven't checked with the bank...let me just... (Will stopped walking and fiddled with the phone) HOLY CRAP! WHERE'D THAT COME FROM?... right... you sold it as is? In what, a couple weeks? Movie rights too? No edits at all? Jeez, man... and you got that much too? And that's just the advance? Wow, That's quite a haul. Thanks, man. What, a book tour? Perfect. Put it off for about eight or twelve weeks... I can take a trip, see something new, and come to it refreshed...See you tomorrow."

Great. More money. Maybe it's time to have some fun with it. But what kind of fun?

As he resumed walking, at a pace fast enough for Harvey, his phone buzzed. "Oh, hey, Harriet... oh, no, that sounds awful... I can see that... of course... can you meet me at my place?... I think I have an idea... right... see you then... remind me what you do for work?... oh, right. I'll see you in a while."

"Jeez, Harv... one of the boys was shot at. She's frantic to get out of the city. Okay if I loan her the cottage?" Harvey looked up at him and wagged the tail enthusiastically. Will wasn't sure if Harvey was responding to the word "cottage", or just being happy because of the walk, so he took the wag as assent. Will's first thought of a plan was going to take some more phone calls, better made while sitting.

Back at the house, Will apologized for being early. "Harriet needs some help. I'm going to see if I can provide it." He dialed the phone. "Hi, Marge... yes, I'm still down in the big bad city... let me talk to John please... Hi, John. Did you ever find that Office Manager you were looking for a few weeks ago? ...Oh, too bad. Well, I might have a candidate for you... ten years Admin Assistant for a small insurance company, looking for a chance to get out of New York City... yeah, right... articulate, smart, good sense of humor... yeah, I considered it... think you could talk to her?... oh, that's terrific. Skype it is. Thanks, dude. She's on her way here, I'll call back in a few."

Amy was curious. "Shipping the new girlfriend out of town?"

"Nah. One of her sons was shot at, with the promise of more to come unless he joined a gang. There have been more shootings near her, so she wants to get out of the city real quick, taking her mom and two boys with. Thought I'd let her use my place upstate for a while, then I remembered John, the local car and truck dealer. He needs somebody to organize the office work. Is there anything cool to drink? Harvey was up for a trot."

Lane had already stood. "One large lemonade coming up."

Amy's nosy nature ventured another inch into the conversation. "So we get to meet Harriet?"

"Sure. Be nice, she's worried."

Lane responded to this one. "Us? We're always nice."

"Right. Well, be extra nice. Please?"

When Harriet arrived, she still seemed a little frazzled. Lane immediately offered a cool drink, but Harriet was focused. "Okay, Will, you said you have an idea. And what does my job have to do with it?"

Will guided her to the couch and explained. "This is Lane, a friend from college, and her daughter Amy. Ladies, this is Harriet, who I met through a local pastor." He turned to Harriet. "First, you need to know that I own a house south of Rome, upstate. Then, know that a friend of mine up there is looking for an Office Manager for his car dealership. What I was thinking is that you could do that job, use my house, and save some money to get a place. The house has three bedrooms, and a bunch of other rooms to have a life in."

Harriet almost broke down. "So you're offering me a job and a house to live in, far away from the city."

"Well, the possibility of a job. If that doesn't come through, there are other jobs in the area."

"Will, you're my fairy godfather. What's it going to cost me?" Lane, Amy and Will all started laughing at the same time. "What's so funny?"

Lane composed herself. "The thought that Will wants something in return. I haven't even been around him that much recently, but I guarantee you that anything he offers is a gift, not a trade. He doesn't want anything back, he wants to give, to make things better for someone he cares about."

Harriet looked at Will. "I guess that's possible. So how do I get this job, fly up for an interview?"

Will was ready. "Nope. Interview by Skype. I have a really fast connection, so there won't be any of that choppy conversation. I just talked to John a few minutes ago, he's waiting for the call."

Harriet stared, still disbelieving. "That lemonade sounds like a good idea after all..." Amy went to get it. Sensing that Harriet needed to calm down some more, Lane changed the subject. "So tell me about your sons. Will isn't good at satisfying our nosiness."

The conversation slowly filled with relaxed smiles, which Will was glad to see. "Ready for your interview?"

"Will! Let the girl have a moment to prepare. Anything you need? No use looking perfect because nobody looks so great on Skype."

"I think I'll just splash some water on my face, run a comb through the brambles here..." pointing to her head. Lane walked her toward the bathroom. Returning, she chided Will on his impatience. Harriet returned looking refreshed. "Ready for my close-up, Mister Demille."

Will set up the computer, made the introduction, and led Lane and Amy into the bedroom. "She'll do fine. I don't know how well John will come across. He's a good guy, though, so there's hope." Lane and Amy scowled at the fact that he wouldn't let them listen at the door.

Eighteen minutes and twenty seconds later, the bedroom door burst open and Harriet flew through it, tackling Will and knocking him back onto the bed. "You angel! You devil! You magic thing you!" She continued shaking him.

Despite wanting nothing more than to hug her, Will asked "Well? Did you get it?"

"Yeah, I got it. John says I've got four months to organize the place, but if I do that I've got a job for as long as I want. Oh, and he said to thank you, from him." The ensuing lip lock was probably not what John had in mind. Not letting Will stand yet, she asked "Are you just doing this to get rid of me? I mean..."

"No. Not at all. You said you wanted to get out of the city, I knew of a way. I have a trip planned in a couple weeks, so I'll be out of the country for up to a month. Then when I get back we'll have a conversation about where this is going, okay?"

Harriet pouted a little, but agreed. "Okay..."

Lane proposed champagne. "I saw a little bottle in the fridge."

Harriet agreed "But just one for me. I have to get back and tell my mom that I'm dragging us all out into the woods."

When the champagne was poured, Will proposed a toast. "May we all have a life free from fear, and full of joy." Amens resounded, and a clink of glasses. Harriet kissed him again, and was nearly out the door.

"Do you need a mover?"

"Nope. James has a big truck. He'll do nearly anything for Jalapeno burgers." And she was gone.

Lane had a thought. "Last night you heal Amy, today you make me feel better, and now you change a woman's life. When does somebody do something for you?"

"Actually, now. I have a vacation arranged for myself. I've wanted to travel, so I'm going to Scotland. Anyone named MacLeish has to visit the old country at some point, right? I'm thinking a couple weeks, a month maybe."

"Wow."

"So I have to ask a favor, Amy. Would you consider staying here while I'm away, and taking care of the place, and Harvey? I'll cover the rent on your place..."

Amy hugged him. "Ho yeah. Go ahead and be my second excuse to not go back to the office."

When the dust settled a bit, Will remembered the Orange Cake. He had promised, gotten some supplies, but not tried his idea for the recipe yet. He went to work.

The first idea was too sweet, the second tasted weird, but the third... the third was worth eating.

8

As the plane started its descent into Aberdeen, Will questioned his sanity. What kind of fruitcake runs off to Scotland for a month? What kind of nutcase leaves Harriet alone in the countryside? Maybe the kind that needs some time to figure out how to build a different life. Kiltore might be the perfect place to do that. Some time alone, a slightly different culture... yeah, it could be just right.

After picking up his large duffel bag at the baggage claim, Will wandered out to Pickup. There was a man standing there with a sign 'Will MacLeish".

"I'm Macleish..."

"Well hello there. I'm Benedict, your driver today."

"Great. Wasn't expecting a limousine."

"Oh, it's not. We'll have to put your bag in the back seat. Have you eaten?"

"Well, that depends if you consider airline food eating."

"Aah, the best of it only staves off the pains of hunger. We'll stop for a bite. Introduce you to a great place the locals like."

"I told Angus MacAddam I'd get to his office first."

"Aye, the cousin's impatient to meet ye. I'll have him meet us for lunch." Benedict took out his cell phone. "Aye, Miriam... I have yer incoming famous writer...have the cousin meet us at The Cullough. Thanks."

"All set. Let's be off." Benedict led the way to a car one would never confuse with a limo. Once packed, he zoomed off. "I like to get out of the urban centers quick, before anyone decides to have an accident with me. I'll drive easier once we're out."

"So, did I hear you call Angus 'cousin'?"

"Aye, that's why he trusted me to meet you. He had a sale, or he would have met you himself. Out of curiosity, what does an accomplished author from the states want with a month in the Scottish countryside?"

"That's easy. I've been writing for twenty-five years, got nothing else done. No family, a tiny circle of friends... at least I have a dog. He's back in New York."

Benedict gave that a minute. "So it's a classic midlife crisis? Wondering what else there could be to life?"

Will hadn't thought of it that way before. "At least I don't have the thought that my life has been wasted. I worked hard and it has paid off. Over fifty books, and a consistent stream of royalties. The first thing I wrote is still trickling something into the coffers. I'm just wondering what else I want, and how to get it."

Benedict grinned. "Well we shall endeavor with all our might to help you hunt down that next good thing. Starting with lunch. Here we be." He pulled into a small parking lot. Inside, a young woman greeted them.

Benedict introduced his guest. "Kathleen, this is..."

"William MacLeish, author of two of my favorite books. A pleasure, sir."

Will sought immediately to dispense with all formality. He could tell that it was not native to this lively young woman. "Will, please. Glad to meet you, Kathleen." His smile had the desired effect.

"What can I get you, Will? Anything we don't have, I'll run and get it."

Sensing that he may have just introduced prey to predator, Benedict intervened. "Now, Kathleen... the man only now got off the plane. He's only here for some good food to cleanse his palate."

Not to be deterred, Kathleen countered. "Never hurts to know who's on the menu... would you like a sandwich, stew, roast or soup then, Will?"

Amused, Will chose. "The plainest local dish you have. As travel broadens the mind, might new flavors broaden the tastebud's appreciations." Kathleen grinned broadly at the poetic turn of phrase. She had always liked poets.

When Angus arrived, he seemed harried. He carried a folder, that he plopped on the table to shake Will's hand. "Mister William MacLeish, we meet at last. It wasn't the easiest request to fulfill, but I've found three possibilities for you." Turning to Kathleen "A small roast beef and cheese please, Kate."

He opened the folder, and spread out the pictures. "This one is attached, but the ones on either side are empty for the month. The second is a classic vacation bungalow, and the third is the gatehouse to an estate, for which this driveway is no longer used. All three within two and one half miles of downtown Kiltore." Satisfied with his schpeel, Angus took a gulp of the water at his place.

Looking over the possibilities, Will found his preference. "The gatehouse: where is the nearest neighbor?"

Angus had to think. "About three quarters of a mile, and that would be the estate." He pulled out a map. "It's here. The family decided they like the approach from the East better. It's a little shorter, straighter. The old drive has been plowed back into the woods and replanted just beyond the gatehouse."

Will thought about it. "Does it have water and electric?"

"Couldn't legally rent it without... has gas, too. I warn ye, it's the most expensive of the three."

"How much?"

Angus' voice dimmed a bit. "Two thousand for the month, if you stay that long. I remember you weren't sure."

"It's an old building, isn't it?"

"Aye, early 1800s, I think. I can get you an exact date if you want."

Will smiled broadly. "No need… if I'm going to have a midlife crisis, I can think of no better place. I'll take it." Will took out his new Bank of Scotland checkbook. "Is that Euros or Pounds?"

Angus was a bit surprised. "Pounds. I would have thought that you might prefer something more modern…"

"But then it would feel modern. I think this will have a better ambiance. Thank you for all that research." Will handed him the check.

Benedict thought of something "Aah, there it is… I've made a list of the places the local populace prefers, three good restaurants, and two pubs." He handed the list to Will.

Angus shook his head. "Didn't come up that you cook, did it?"

Will chuckled "No, it did not."

"I had a local chef watch your morning show appearance and recommend some groceries. They'll arrive this afternoon, with a fresh set of pots, dishes, et cetera."

"I think I'll keep Benedict's list, though. Nice to have someone else cook once in a while."

As they left, Kathleen came to Will with a small bag. "Pastry, sweet ones for those afternoon munchies. I know you're here for some alone time, but could I invite you here for dinner Saturday at eight?"

Will nodded. "Thank you. I appreciate that. Lunch was excellent, I look forward to dinner." He kissed her hand.

Angus felt it necessary to warn him. "She's going to drag you out for a pub crawl. You can call Ben or myself any time for a ride home."

Ben agreed. "Aye."

Will shook his head. "I don't think that will be necessary. Besides, no cell phone."

Ben was horrified. "Aah! We must stop and get you one. Reception is good from Aberdeen to Inverrary, gets a little spotty once you get into the hills. But for local calls like that, indispensable."

"No, Ben. Thank you for the thought, but I would like to go old-school this month. I didn't even bring a computer, only a notebook and pen. Mostly, I'll be breathing this fine clear air, hiking in nature, and contemplating my place in the world. Besides, I'll know my way back, and I can walk."

Ben didn't want to, but he accepted the preference. "Well, alright, I guess."

When the group arrived at the gatehouse, Will was delighted. The stone pillars at the entrance were intact, and about twenty yards of eight foot stone wall led away from either side of the spectacular wrought-iron gates, still hanging from the pillars. Just inside the gates, The Gatehouse. "Wow. It looks even better than the pictures!"

Angus showed the place, not fully convinced that Will would love it. "There's only the kitchen, sitting room, bed and bath, could that be enough?"

"Oh, Angus... it's almost too much. You know of Henry Thoreau?" Two more bedrooms, and Harriet and the boys would be comfortable too.

"Aye..."

"I'm a great fan. The cabin he used at Walden Pond was the size of this one room. I'll consider that someone has lent me a castle." He plopped down his large duffel. "Is there a key?"

Angus shrugged his shoulders. Not like any other American he had met. "Here you are... and I hope the ghosties don't take to frightening ye."

"Any ghost with the good taste to show up here... I hope they're good conversationalists. Thank you so much." Angus and Ben left at mid-afternoon.

At four o'clock, two vehicles pulled in the driveway. The first was a delivery van. "Kitchen goods and groceries for a William MacLeish..."

"That's me..."

"Hello Mister MacLeish! I am Connor Land, head chef at The Garden. I've got the honor to supply you. Angus showed us your TV appearance. If you need a larger kitchen, come to The Garden any time. I tried your quick Onion Soup recipe, and it's now on our menu. Everyone loves it." The man was about forty, and athletic. The truck was full of goodies.

As Connor and his assistant unloaded the van, the occupant of the second vehicle, a Land Rover, approached. A very well-dressed woman who seemed to be between forty and sixty. Will always had a problem guessing women's ages. "Greetings, Mister MacLeish. I am Anna Campbell, from the estate house. I heard that you were a writer, and thought you might like a writing desk. Unused at the manse, I'm afraid, but if you would like..." A man was pulling a writing desk appropriate to Will Shakespeare from the back of the Rover.

"Oh my... that's beautiful. I hadn't planned to write much while here, but this desk could change my plans. Thank you."

She smiled. "Good. Let's find a spot for it, shall we?" Inside, Connor and his crew couldn't find spaces for everything. Will sought to unconfuse them.

"Just the one frying pan, two pots and the small Dutch oven. Four place settings and some mugs. The cups and saucers, I'm not likely to use." He opened the refrigerator, which they had stuffed to the gills. "Oh heavens... I'm only here for a month. You should have this, this, and that back. I know it's odd, but you should take back those teabags I see. Do you have some loose tea, maybe a Darjeeling, or something Chinese?"

Connor grinned. "There's the loose tea in the cupboard, a selection of them. Davis, take the large cuts of meat, we'll leave four full place settings, and be out of your way Mister..."

"Please... everyone should call me Will. Your generosity is fantastic, but a little too much. I had thought to be merely another tourist, quieter than most. Sort of invisible."

Anna informed him. "We Scots consider writers a national treasure. Storytellers of your caliber are celebrated and honored guests. I think you'll find a great many fans here, and I'm afraid you'll have to put up with being a celebrity. If they find you here and become bothersome, you are welcome at the manse, on the other side of the wood. The original drive will provide a walkable path."

Will could tell they were disappointed. "I'm sorry for that outburst. I thank you sincerely, but I think I need a nap. I can never sleep on airplanes."

"Oh gracious. We've caught you in the throes of jet lag. Come, gentlefolk, I think a day or three of peace is in order to let Will adjust." All three shook his hand, smiling as they left. Will had one more thing to do before succumbing to the exhaustion he was starting to feel.

He dialed for an international operator. "Hello...I would like to call New York, and arrange to put calls from this number on my American Express account for the next thirty days... Yes maam... the card number is... yes, that is the black card... thank you..." Will dialed the number for his place in Soho. The answering machine. "Hi, Amy... Just called to let you know I've landed, in one piece and with all my luggage. Bye." Five minutes later, the quiet had lulled Will to sleep on the couch.

At midnight, Will drifted awake. Seeing stars through the window, he wandered out to sit on a small bench beside the door. Breathing the Scottish atmosphere for a while, phrases started popping up in his mind.

At night the hills exude a scent of green.

The souls venture out

I am in this sacred place by invitation

A guest welcome to tell the tale.

It occurred to Will that he hadn't written much poetry, and that he might have found the right place to practice that highest and best use of language. Then he realized that he must be half asleep, because he had never even thought in such terms before. He went inside hoping that he could remember the poem he had written in his head. Fortunately, it was still there waiting for his slow, meticulous handwriting to record it. Then he went back to bed.

No-one saw Will until 7:30 Saturday, when he stopped in the flower shop for a gift for his date. The man who helped him asked who his date was with. Hearing that it was Kathleen, his face went all wise. "Watch yourself, Mister MacLeish, that girl will wear you out with the dancing 'til dawn..."

Will was amused. "Yes, she seems a very outgoing girl. Do you know what flowers she might like?"

"Aye, Wildflowers, with some thistle among them. Bit of a wildflower herself."

"A nice big fistful, then. This date's just for dinner, but I appreciate the invitation."

"Just dinner, you think? You'll be lucky to get home by midnight. Here you go, sir... and good luck to you." He handed Will a large group of wildflowers.

"Thanks. That should do it."

When Will wandered through the door of the restaurant, Kathleen was serving an older couple. She dropped their plates and swept over to him. "And who's all that for?"

"What other heart should I bring the whole countryside to impress? As everything this fine day of early summer, for thee, lady."

"Oh kind sir, I am but your humble servant. Let me recommend the booth in the corner, while I find appropriate vases for your kind gift." She danced off into the kitchen, holding the flowers close, as if they were magic.

Will found a spot in the recommended booth, and Kathleen returned in moments. "They're gorgeous. Thank you. They're in the back until I can get them home. So, Mister William MacLeish, what's your pleasure? There are roasts galore, fresh vegetables and greens from nearby plots..."

"It occurs to me that I've never had Haggis. Whatever goes with that might be a fine idea."

"Never?"

"Never."

Kathleen ran to the back, coming out with a small plate. "Best to test the flavor before signing up for more. Some don't enjoy it."

Having read how to consume Haggis, Will took a piece of flatbread and scooped up a bit. "Hmmm... like a dinner Pate. Fantastic."

Kathleen was impressed. "Haggis dinner, coming up!" She waved to the waiter. "I told the boss that I was off the clock as soon as you arrived." To the waiter "Two Haggis dinners. Salad first, Brandied Cobbler after."

Will felt that a disclaimer was in order. "I have to confess, I might not be a great date. Last time I had a dinner out with a beautiful woman was, oh that's right, three weeks ago. Before that was about ten years ago." He felt a little guilty for almost forgetting Harriet.

"Ten years? How in the world did you manage that, what with the New York girls chasin' you down the street?"

"I live a couple hours north of the city, just go in to meet with my agent. The rest of the time I've been writing, alone in my cottage. Actually, that's a situation I hope to find a way out of, writing all the time. It gets to feeling like a monastery sometimes. I think I could benefit from some more people. Maybe a family."

By the time the cobbler landed in front of them, Kathleen knew exactly what she wanted to do. "I have an idea."

"Yeah?"

"You are looking for more practice with people, and I would like to have something better than a one-nighter connection with my new famous friend. I think that three days a week I should drag you out to things. Not always a date. Maybe a birthday party, a football match, some music. I could be your guide. You get your time to think, I get to have more fun for however long you're here. What do you think?"

It took Will a moment to absorb the concept. "Sure. Could be twice a week, though… don't want to overdo it. When do we start?"

After a mouthful of dessert, Kathleen responded. "Now. We finish this, and go to the pub. I have an idea there."

Once in the Oak and Thistle Public House, Kathleen scanned for the people she needed. She found them at a corner table, six men over 60 years old murmuring among themselves while playing cards.

"Gentlemen! Just the group for a plan I have."

One of the men looked up. "Uh oh, James, we're in for it now…"

"Not at all. How would you like to keep a good thing from the tourists?"

That woke the boys up. "By doing what, exactly?"

Kathleen pulled two chairs up to the table. "Here, we have William MacLeish, a writer from across the pond. He's here for some quiet time to think, and to experience a place he's never been, and meet some people he hasn't met. If the tourists find out he's here, the pub gets too crowded, and he gets no thinking done."

"What's our part?"

"In case anyone recognizes him, he's my cousin Will from Manchester. We include him in some things, a football match, a picnic, any of the calmer normal things we do all the time. Treat him like a visiting relative, not a famous person."

The man with the most color left in his hair spoke first. "Well first, you'll need a drink for this. Pleased to meet you, Will MacLeish, I am Devon MacAndrew. What'll ye have?"

Will decided. "That bit in your glass looks good…"

Then Kathleen. "Me too. This mean you'll help?"

"Aye, and what else that's so much fun were we doing? This is going to take a plan. First, a new name. All great cover stories start with the name. I think Manchester is wrong. Somewhere like Philadelphia in the States would work easier. Some name like… um…"

Will thought to help. "My daughter calls me Aidan."

One of the others chimed in. "… MacLeod!"

"Aye. Glad to meet you, Aidan MacLeod." Approval made its way around the table. "And that way, you can be a fourth cousin, here to see the old country." He made a motion to the bartender, and a round of drinks appeared. "

The eldest of the gents at the table finally spoke. "Of course, there's another possibility altogether."

"And what would that be, Mister MacDougal?"

"The man could be himself, and just not advertise the famous writer aspect. We have had royalty and celebrities here before, and nary a problem. I don't see that this time should be any different. Princess Diana spent a week here, and walked about without a fuss. You see, Mister MacLeish, we Scots are a naturally quiet group, not given to intrusive actions. You might be recognized, but just with a hello or the shake of your hand."

Will nodded. "If you think I can get away with it, I like that even better. I wouldn't need the security detail Princess Diana had."

The older man took a drink and nodded. "Actually, I think we are going to need a story, if you have one. Storytelling is a time-honored activity in pubs. You can add to the flavor of the place."

Kathleen reached into her purse and pulled out a volume of Will's short stories. "Now, gents, you know not all writers know their stories off the top of their heads. You can read from this, Will."

Will took the book and leafed through. "Oh, here's one... not very long, and I've since thought of another, better ending. And I know it well enough not to read it. A short one okay?"

Everyone agreed, so Will started. "Jameson Trotter was, he thought, a boring man..." As he spoke, the entire story unfolded in his mind and he made a few edits. Ten minutes and half minutes and a beer later, Will spoke the final line "Jameson Trotter decided to go ahead and be a truly boring man."

The table erupted in raucous laughter, and pounding on the table. "Good one, old son. Well done!" In the corner, a fiddler started to play.

"Some dancing, Will?"

Will thought to object, but then he recognized the intro to a familiar slow song. Slow dancing he could do. Two reels and a jig later, Will fell into a chair, worn out. "I haven't danced so much in decades! Sorry I'm out of shape."

Kathleen wasn't disappointed. "Not every man half your age would have done as much. You should have a break, a pint, and we'll see if you're ready to do something more."

"More?"

"Like a walk or a cab ride home."

"Oh. That second one is probably a fine thought. I haven't had this much to drink recently, either." At the end of the beer, Will's eyelids started to droop. Kathleen put him in a cab and kissed his cheek.

"Good night, ye good man."

Sunday turned up with a light drizzle at six o'clock. The right atmosphere for some oatmeal and a sausage, with a small pot of dark tea. Oh good, there's Orange Pekoe. It took forty-five minutes to soften the oatmeal, being the old-fashioned type, but the result was worth it. Will added some butter and cinnamon. Thank Connor for the spices, and for the right size of teapot. Have to get to the Garden restaurant soon. Have to bring Harriet and the boys here some day. They'd enjoy that.

As Will was finishing his pot of tea, he noticed that the rain had stopped, and the sun was out. Maybe having fueled himself, it was time to explore Kintore. Take the camera, just in case. Fortunately, he had transferred the more private of Harriet's pictures to a password-protected file on his computer.

Bit of a hike into town after all, the two Scottish miles feeling very different from two miles on a treadmill. It was nine o'clock when Will arrived at the edge of downtown Kintore. The first outdoor chairs he saw were at The Cullough, he sat for a minute before starting to walk again. The waiter surprised him.

"What can I get you, sir?" A tall man stood behind Will, pad in hand.

"Ah, maybe a coffee and a pastry?"

"Danish, Puff or Scone?"

Sounded like a good idea to Will. "If they're not very large, a Danish and a Scone, please. I'll be exploring the town with my friend this morning." He held up the camera.

"Yes, sir... would you like the large Coffee American then?"

"Oh, just black coffee."

"Yes sir. Back in a very few minutes."

Will was amazed. He hadn't expected the place to be open. He expressed that to the waiter.

"No, sir, technically we're not open. I'm the only one here. Thought you looked like you could use a little something."

Will had picked up some of the local vernacular already. "Aye, you're right about that. I hope this will cover it." He handed the man a five-pound note.

"Aah, that and much more. I'll be back with your change."

"No, you keep that. Dedication should be rewarded."

"Well then thank you, good sir! Are you in town for a few days?"

"Actually, might be a month. This visit is what some would call my mid-life crisis. I'm trying to think of what to do next."

"Aah, I wish you luck. Such choices can drive a man to the drink, and thus indecision."

The waiter smiled and went back inside. After his treat, Will waved toward him in the window and headed off to discover Kintore. What he found was a photogenic mix of old and new. At one small church, he knocked on the rectory door and asked if he could take a few pictures of the interior. Services were due to start soon, and the pastor invited him back in the afternoon.

As he wandered down one street, he saw an older man walking toward him and had an idea. "Excuse me, sir... could I ask a favor?"

"Aye..."

"I am trying to get used to my new camera. Could I take a picture of you?"

The man seemed amused. "Can't think why you would want such a challenge. The wife says there are no good pictures of me. But if you like, ye may. What shall I do?"

Will was delighted. "I'll go back a little, and you can just walk toward me, like you were."

"Aye."

Once Will took the picture and looked at what he had, he exclaimed. "Wow, this thing is good!"

The man came to see. "Aah, that's a fine photo. D'ye think I could get a print for the wife? She might get jealous not to have one so good of herself."

Will was flattered. "Sure. Is there somewhere that could print it for us?"

"I'm thinking the computer store might do that, tell them ye want to see how good the printers are..."

"Good plan." They started walking. Hadn't gotten three steps when two pre-teen girls came up to them.

"Taking pictures? Could you take one of us?"

Will looked around for the perfect backdrop. "Okay, how about in front of that store?" The girls were very excited, and agreed. In a couple minutes, Will took the shot he was trying for, and showed them. As girls will do, they squealed with delight. "Did I hear you say sommat about getting a print? Could we have one?"

Will was wondering why all the fuss. The pictures were clear and well composed, but not much more than that. "Sure. Come along with us." Once in the computer store, Will explained to the salesman, and handed him the memory card from the camera, pointing out his subjects who were pretending to look at laptops. The salesman nodded, and went to his best printer.

"With this model, you don't need a computer. Insert the card here, select a size, select a photo, and push 'Print'"

Will followed instructions, and the printer spat out the prints. Quite satisfactory, as far as he could tell. The salesman was more impressed than that. "Ach! Could we use a print of this to show off the printer?"

Will supposed he should ask the subject, and motioned him over.

"So now I'm a model? Aah, go ahead then. Ye've my permission."

That made the salesman happy. He made a few adjustments with the printer, and pressed the button. "We'll have this mounted and hanging over the printer that made it in a couple of days. Thank you Mister MacLeish, and Mister…"

Will's first subject almost laughed as he said "MacLeish. Daniel MacLeish. Call me Dan" Will thanked the salesman, and everyone wandered out of the store with their prints. Dan suggested that his wife would like to meet Will "If you have a minute", and Will nodded.

Dan's wife Mary was at the checkout of a store when Dan pointed her out. Will had an inspiration and set the camera. He caught her coming out the door, bags in hand, when she saw her husband and smiled.

Dan introduced them, showing her the photograph Will had taken. She hugged Will, and invited him for lunch. "This is the MacLeish territiory, did ye know? This area around Aberdeen for some fifty miles. Fewer and fewer these days, but to me everyone with the name is a cousin. You must have been taking portraits for a long time, eh?"

Will was a little embarrassed. "Not really. I took some pictures in my teens, and I guess the basics stayed with me. I was trying to get some experience with my new camera when I met Dan."

Mary decided she was jealous. "So how can I convince you to take my portrait, to hang beside his?"

"Oh... I already did." Will turned to the picture of Mary coming out of the store. "It's when you saw this nice fella. I think that might be the best smile I've seen."

She stared at the picture for a minute, and handed the camera back. "You've made me look young!"

Will disagreed. "Not I, but your connection to your husband. I just caught the glint in your eyes."

"Aah, you're a Scot in the truest sense there, Will. I bet you've talked your way into a few hearts, the way you speak." Mary deflected the compliment.

After lunch, Will promised to have Mary's portrait printed and bring it by before four, and wandered off to do the church interiors. When he got there, the pastor was glad to see him return.

"Not many tourists stop by our little chapel. How did you come to us?"

Will wasn't sure. "I was taking some pictures of the town, for the folks back home, and I walked down your street. The front of the building seemed classical, so I took a picture. It was a pretty good bet the inside would be beautiful as well. Is the church very old?"

"Four hundred years, hasn't missed a Sacrament yet."

"Wow. That's terrific. Would you like copies of the pictures once I've taken them?"

"Aah, that would be quite kind. Right through this door, and I'll leave you to it. The church secretary will be in the office, but I have a parishioner to visit."

Will walked through the door and smiled. Just as he had thought, the light through the stained glass, the old-fashioned altar facing the Crucifix... this was going to be fun. Forty-five minutes and as many photos later, he sat in the first pew to see what he had. Very satisfied, he stood up as the church secretary came through the door.

"Mister MacLeish? I wondered if you fell asleep."

"Oh, I can imagine falling into a meditative state in such beauty, but it gives me energy. Here, see what I've caught." He handed her the camera. "Just swipe right or left to page through."

"Oh my. They're wonderful. Pastor said we could have copies?"

"Yes, indeed. Have a computer handy?"

They went into the office, and she copied the files from his memory card. "Are you a church- going man, Mister MacLeish?"

"Not so much. I did grow up Catholic, and I'm glad to say I've taken the lessons into the rest of my life, but I rarely attend Mass. I have to say, there's something more than architecture that makes this church beautiful. If I've captured any of that I'd be glad."

The woman had encountered this before. "What the New Age congregants call 'Sacred Space', right?"

"Yes. That's it... something about this place, and the church accents it, amplifies it."

"I'm so glad when people notice. May I invite you to Mass next Sunday? We usually have an eight o'clock and a ten o'clock service."

"I'll have to consider that. Oh look at the time... I promised someone to do an errand. Thank you for access, and maybe I'll see you again."

As he left, she muttered "Blessed be the wind that could carry you here, William."

Back at Dan's house, Will presented Mary with her portrait. "Oh, Will... I've never seen such beauty in myself. Thank you so much."

"Well, it's nice to think that I have relatives here. Not so many back at home."

Dan came in to the room. "Are your parents still around?"

"Yes, still in the house I grew up in. They won't let me do much for them, though, now that I can."

Mary knew the answer to this syndrome. "One doesn't have children so they'll do things for you. Probably the only thing they want is to see you, to know what's going on in your life, to know that you're happy and well. That's the ultimate reward. When you go back, visit. Tell them the story of your life."

Will blushed. "I will. And I'll appreciate the birthday card with the five dollar bill in it. Maybe I can cook for them someday."

"Aah, ye cook?" Dan was delighted. "Ye can always practice on us, if ye like."

Mary scolded the old man. "Now Daniel, you're already quite well fed..." She tapped the slightly convex part of his front. Will took his leave, at least for the day, promising to visit again.

9

On his way back to the Gatehouse, Will wondered about photography. Did he want to do it for money? Possibly. Did he want a portrait studio? Maybe not. Wandering around with the camera and meeting people was fun, though. Maybe add in a phone or something to be able to email people their pics on the spot. More fun if the 'something' would allow for a little Photoshop action before emailing.

Will let the thought sink in. The walk back to the gatehouse would leave him enough sink-in time, so that by the time he sat at his kitchen table, he would know if it was a probability. The thought made him smile. As he passed The Cullough, he sat. Having been on his feet for a few hours, a break seemed in order.

Kathleen came out the front door. "William! What brings you back?"

"I need a break before walking back. I've been being a tourist, taking some pictures. Do you work every day or what?"

"Oh, I cover for the other wait staff sometimes. Can I get you anything?"

"A mug of coffee sounds good..."

"I'll be right back with that. Coffee black, right?" She made a face, not being able to imagine why a person would take the sugar and cream out of their coffee. When she returned, Will had a question.

"So what is a Cullough, anyway?"

"A brave man. A bit of a brag on behalf of the clan. Your last name is more interesting, I think."

"Oh? What could my name mean?"

"MacLeish is a contraction of 'Son of the Servant of God' in Gaelic. Your people came from the Hebrides, settled here and in between farming and fishing were part of bringing Christianity to Scotland. Makes me wonder if the next part of your life could be religious."

Will tugged at his nonexistent beard. "Well, I can talk to people about such things when I get around to it, but I think I'd rather set an example than convert people. A life led in peace is the best advertisement, I think."

Kathleen found this fascinating. "You've thought about it."

"Sure. And I think all my books reflect the attitude somewhere in them. I just don't think I could let someone else tell me what to think. Authority issues, I guess." Sensing that the conversation was going to run out of steam, he changed the subject. "How about you? Anything you dream of doing?"

"A family. Finding a nice fella and settle in for the long haul."

"There must have been possibilities…"

"Oh sure, and near misses, but not that I could commit to. Seems like the kind of thing a person should be sure of."

"Yeah. I have to confess, that's one of the pictures I would fall for."

After a moment of silence, Will changed the subject. "Hey, if you have a day off, how about we make it a tourist day? A couple castles, a couple towns, a little natural splendor? Most people who live in tourist destinations never get to see the sights..."

Kathleen was not amused. "Run around with a hundred other tourists hoping for a glance at something they've never seen? I don't see the attraction."

"No, I was thinking to hire a car and driver, go where we want when we want. I think I should take some more pictures."

Kathleen grinned. "That does sound like more fun... what the heck, let's do that. I have Wednesday open."

"Wednesday, then, nice and early. Right now, I should go and rest my weary ancient bones."

"Early indeed. There's a spot in the Highlands to watch the sun rise over a loch. How's that for natural splendor?"

"Fantastic. Leave at five?"

"Six will do it. Then breakfast, then a castle. I'll be here at six on Wednesday."

Will was becoming more and more impressed with her. "Then so shall I, sweet lady." He kissed her hand and swept away as if transported on a cloud of romantic dreams. Once he arrived at the gatehouse, he called for the car. Three hundred pounds for the day, and a driver who knows all the good places, and how to avoid the mobs.

That's good. Now two days of quiet reflection, that experience he came here for. He imagined a stern voice in his head demanding that he choose something. Now, now, NOW!

After a good sleep Sunday night, Will awoke with a sense of purpose. Gulping down a fine breakfast of a little bit of everything, he sat at the writing desk. In his notebook, he wrote down everything he knew of that could be worth having in a life. He wound up with one hundred and twelve items, of which he meant to select the four to six most important.

He circled 'House', 'Wife with a sense of humor' and 'Community', so they would not get crossed out. It only took him an hour to eliminate everything else but 'Art", which he supposed could include writing.

To fill the rest of the day, there were drawings to do. He could imagine a line of two dozen greeting cards based on the photographs of Kintore.

Tuesday morning, the phone rang. "Hello?... Oh, hi, Kathleen...no, that's okay, what's up?... oh wow, your mom's sick...oh, I'm sorry... want some company? ... of course. Take care of the family. I'm sure they will appreciate having you there... yeah... I'll see you when you get back... if you change your plans, just call. I'll be there...right...See you when we can... oh, can I ask you something... is there a bookstore in town?... great, the street I didn't see Sunday...Thanks, Kathleen."

So that left Tuesday and Wednesday open. Having filled too many pages of his notebook with sketches, Will thought he would look for an art supply store. Sometimes, he remembered, bookstores have such things over in a corner. Maybe some drawing paper a little larger than the notebook.

On the way to town, Will noticed a tree sticking out at the edge of a field. It seemed solitary and photogenic there, so he stopped and took some pictures with his now-omnipresent camera. When he got to town, he headed directly to the bookstore. Kintore Bookseller was a small storefront on a street of buildings from the early 1900s. Wandering in, he was greeted by the familiar smell of books, and the voices of two women. "Hello".

"Hi. I'm in town on vacation, thought I'd stop in." The women went back to tending the store. It only took a few minutes to browse the two aisles of books. "It's a fine store you have... very friendly." Will thought the compliment would be well-received.

"Thank you. Get something while you can, though. No telling how long we can keep it open."

"Oh, slow sales?"

"No sales. I guess the book has had its day."

The second woman chimed in. "Don't mind my sister. True, sales have been slow, but we'll think of something. I'm Elizabeth Adams, my sister and I own the place. And you are... Oh my God! You're MacLeish! William MacLeish! The author of all those books! I've seen your video on the net! Oh gosh I guess that news surprised some folks..."

"Yes. There has been some resentment, some joy, and a few more sales as people get used to the idea. I've got a new one coming out in a couple months."

The first woman approached, blushing. "Sorry for the downer reception, Mister MacLeish. I'm Donna, the dour sister."

Will reached into his encouragement file. "Aah, nothing dour about ye. I still see a spark in your eye, and I know that bookshops around the world are suffering. How can I help?"

Elizabeth exclaimed the first thing that came to mind. "Would you consider a book signing, if you're here long enough?"

Will was delighted. "I'll go you one better. I'll order up the first copies and have the release party here."

"AAAgh! There's not enough room here for such a thing! I'd love it, but..."

"Maybe there's a hall we could borrow? If you have a computer available, I can contact my agent, to see what's needed."

"Aye, there..." Donna pointed to a desk.

Will felt fired up. He had a cause. He typed the email with four fingers, hunting and pecking. "Hey Seamus... what would it take to have the Release Party here in Kintore? Can we get some pre-release copies for the bookstore here? Please respond to this address." He thought for a moment. "Oh... the subject line. I have to put 'Will-o-matic' so he knows it's me." He looked at his watch. "Oh... five hours earlier there, he's just waking up. I think we can arrange for you to sell the new book a week or two before anyone else. That might give sales a boost."

"That would be marvelous. Thank you, Mister MacLeish."

"And that would be Will, to my friends. Seamus will do his usual magical thing and get back to us in about four hours. Meanwhile, I have another chore or two. You two keep the faith, and I'll be back this afternoon.

....

This was Will's big chance to make up to Connor Land for his tantrum upon arrival in Kintore. The Garden restaurant was a lovely modern place, with the smells of roasted meats and pastries right inside the door. Then Connor came over. "Hi, Will, come to do some cooking?" He shook Will's hand as if they were long-lost brothers.

"Actually, no. Thought I'd let someone else cook. Here to eat. Hope there's a seat..."

Connor laughed. "For you, we would throw out some customers. Fortunately, we don't have to. Here, this is my favorite spot: near the kitchen, but at a window. What would you like? We can make it up. I was thinking some Gaspacho and a grilled cheese with ham for myself."

"Ooh... that sounds great. Do you do onion rings?"

"Best in the land!"

"Add some of those and a juice..."

"We have a nice vegetable juice that we make here. Not too thick, not too thin..."

"Perfect."

Connor had a big grin on his face. "I'll be back with that. Mind if I join you?"

"Aah, the good company that makes a meal a meal. Of course, please do." It took Connor less than ten minutes to return with a cart full of lunch. Will was surprised.

"So you're a fast food establishment!"

"Not exactly. We have a fellow on the grill with a gift for timing things at a higher temperature. So grilled things don't take long at all." He distributed the food, and took the cart back toward the kitchen. Sitting down, Connor wanted to know something. "So how are you getting along with the vacation and your sparsely outfitted kitchen?"

Will chuckled. "I tell you, that gatehouse seems like a palace, and everything you brought over is perfect. And the vacation is super. I did want to take a break, sort of do nothing, and I'm in the perfect place to do that. All the time to think, and just breathe that I could ask for. The schedule I had been keeping of three books a year, well that used up all my time. I wanted to find some balance."

Connor nodded. "Three? That might be like me trying to run three restaurants by myself, and I have my hands full with the one."

"Right. Maybe I could do a little writing, but have time for a social life, maybe a family. Plus, I just discovered a penchant for portrait photography. Maybe I'll do something with that. Oh, this Gaspacho is terrific. Think I'll shut up and eat."

Connor halfway through a bite of his sandwich, gave a thumbs up. "Do you miss New York in our somewhat sleepy village?"

"Nah, miss the people, though. I found out about a month ago that I have a daughter. It's been great fun getting to know her."

"Aye, daughters are fun. I've two of them, eight and eleven." The rest of the lunch proceeded with little else than an occasional yummy sound or a nod from either man.

When both were finished and through a cup of tea, Will excused himself. "I'm bound back to the bookstore. Trying to arrange to have the launch party for my latest opus here in Kintore. Oh, I was thinking of getting some art supplies. Does someone in town sell pens and drawing paper?"

"Aye, Brown's Stationers. On the High Street, an old dark gray storefront. They look empty from the street, but inside's full of supplies. Good luck with everything! Come again soon... next time I'll actually let you pay." A hearty handshake and two big smiles, and Will was off.

....

Back at the bookshop, Donna and Elizabeth were glad to see him. "No response yet... are you sure you had the right address?"

Will frowned. "Been using the same one for twenty years. Not like him to not get back to me, even just to say he got the message. I think I'll hurry back to the gatehouse and make some phone calls." Looking at the Sent Mail file, he had the right address. "I'll let you know what I find. See you soon, ladies."

He was almost out the door when Elizabeth called him back. "Here's something! Will!"

Will opened the e-mail and read aloud. "I'll work on it. Go back to your vacation and stop thinking up things for me to do." He chuckled. "Yes, that's sort of what I expected. Busy man, but he finds time for his writers. I'll tell him to go ahead and send any news to you, and tell me when I get back to New York." Typing in his message, Will felt some pride that he might be able to help. If his idea didn't pan out, he would still arrange for a few hundred copies free to the store.

Hugs and laughter ensued, after which Will actually left. Walking down the street, he was surprised how easily he could interact with people he had never met. The question remained in his thoughts of whether this is what people do on vacation.

On his way to the cottage for some more rest and contemplation, there was Kathleen. Will admitted to himself that she looked better working than most models looked when posing. He waved, but she did not see him. He continued walking.

Will also continued thinking. Was Kathleen the answer? A house, a couple kids and Kathleen? The picture wasn't clear enough at the moment. The picture was a familiar one... of course! Harriet, the house and a couple of kids! He wasn't running away from the picture. He already had the one he wanted. It was time to go tell her so. Questions about what to do with his life would solve themselves. He needed to see the folks, then be there for Harriet. That's all he wanted.

Back at the cottage, silence was a familiar thing. Like the silence at his house in the country. So what does one do for the best advice? Call mom. "Hi, mom... yes, I'm in Scotland trying to think of what to do next with my life.

"You know, where to take it... yeah... I have two places to live, and enough money to be comfortable... not a fortune, but with a modest life I'm not likely to go broke... right... hey, can I come talk to you and dad about this, maybe get some advice about how to decide? I'd certainly appreciate it... I can be there tomorrow afternoon... oh, okay, the next day.

"We can spend the day together... I can tell you a good story of my recent life...I know it's been a long time, and I apologize for that, It's my fault... so fixated on what I was doing... thanks, mom... see you in a couple days. Bye."

Will guessed that Kathleen was his next stop. He left a message on her cell phone that she should meet him after work. She would probably check her phone before the dinner rush.

Then there were three more people to talk to: Lane, Seamus and Harriet. He let them know that he would be back in the country soon, and tried to keep it sounding casual.

At 10:00 that night, Kathleen wandered into The Oak & Thistle, looking a little worn. "Hey... rough shift?"

"Aye... it was a night for customers to argue; with one another, with the menu, with their bill, with the way things were cooked..." She paused and looked Will straight in the eye. "You're here to tell me that you're not staying." Then she smiled. "It's someone you can't stop thinking about. You have to get back to her."

Will looked down at the table. "But how do you know? If I stayed, I would always feel like a visitor."

Kathleen smiled. "Whoever she is, she's lucky. Her absence lives in your eyes. Everyone but you can see it. As to feeling like a visitor, I guess I get that. We'll miss you. Coming back some time?"

"Yes. I'll probably be here around March 10th, to launch sales of my latest book. Kintore Books needs some more sales, and that ought to help."

Kathleen didn't speak for a minute. "So I guess I'll see you then."

Will felt guilty. "Sorry we didn't turn into a romance. I just can't."

"Aah no, mustn't be sorry, I'm only glad to have met ye. Now I can say I know a famous author who's a good man. I'll go now, so I can sleep. Tomorrow's another day..." She stood, and kissed his forehead, then she was gone.

10

When his cab pulled up to his childhood home, Will sighed. How different would it have been, he wondered, if he had stayed here and had a life?

His mother interrupted that thought. "William!" She ran to the curb and hugged him. "You seem well... a little thinner maybe. Let's get your bags up to your room, you're staying here tonight so we get a whole day tomorrow."

Will didn't argue. He would take all of mom's hugs he could get. Once inside, Dad spoke up. "Hey, stranger... good to see you. Mom says you're looking for advice."

"Yes, sir."

Dad grinned. "Don't take any wooden nickels." Dad advice: priceless. Will hugged his father, who hugged him back. "Don't stay away so long. It worries your mother."

"I won't."

"I suppose you're old enough for a beer, if you would like one."

Will cocked his head. "I am, but some iced tea would be better. The air in the plane was dry."

Dad nodded. "No sugar, as I remember."

"Right. That's great."

Mom pulled Will down onto the sofa. "So tell us... we heard about the sixty books, and getting mugged in Central Park, but what's behind it all? Details, man. Mommy wants details." When dad came back with the iced tea, mom and dad lened toward him, listening.

An hour later, mom stood up. "Lunch in an hour and a half. I'll leave you with my boyfriend here, and be back after lunch to contradict everything he says."

Dad left it a moment then asked "So what does this Harriet look like?" Will took out his cell phone and showed him. "Wow. Kind of irresistible."

Will filled in some more detail. "And smart and kind and easy to talk to, and listen to."

Dad paused, and looked at him. "You know, when I met your mom I thought she was incredibly beautiful. She was out of my league, but I thought she might go out with me anyway. Every time I saw her, I smiled. Still do.

"Point is, you can react to your first impression. You might wind up with a terrific partner and a great life. Before we were married, I was being very impressed by the whole 'death do we part' thing. I talked to the priest who married us. He said something surprising. 'Don't think of it as the rest of your life. Think of it as maybe a year. That's easier. Can you commit for the next year to be faithful and loving to this woman?'

"So if you're wondering what to do, think in smaller chunks of time. If you think of doing one thing for the rest of your life, you'll never do anything. Think of a new activity in chunks of a few months, that you'll try it. From what you've said, I'd advise you to go out to your house in the country and live with her. Get to know her. Then if you can commit to a year, you'll probably be fine.

"No guarantees, but I've been married a long time. Appreciate your life one moment, one day at a time. Stop looking for fifty years. Life comes in moments. It leads us on hour by hour, day by day."

After some silence, dad asked "That enough advice for the moment?"

"Yeah, dad, and it's probably the best I'll get."

"How about a walk? It's how I hide my smoking from your mom."

"Sure. I've been sitting too much lately, then I fell asleep on the plane and woke up with a stiff neck, too."

"Irene! We're going for a walk!

"Okay. Back in an hour, please!"

"Right!" The fellas left for a round of 'Who still lives here?' Will was suitably impressed that he recognized more than half the neighbors. One of them invited the two MacLeish men in for a beer, which invitation was gleefully accepted. The price of the beer was a recounting of Will's adventure with amnesia. The full version required four beers each.

Arriving home for lunch, their alcohol content was called into question. "Peter MacLeish, you've been drinking, and roped your son into it too!"

"Now Andrea... a couple beers with a neighbor is just a sociable thing to do. Bill wanted to know what happened with Will..."

"Bill Jackson, I might have known. The two of you might as well be a drinking club. Well never mind. I've made some nice tuna sandwiches for lunch, and there are potato chips. That ought to absorb some of the alcohol. Sit and eat." Mom kept muttering to herself, something about how easily the men in her life are lured to excess.

The afternoon and the next day were filled with conversation, parent portraits, chess, horseshoes and both his parents beating Will at pocket billiards on the table they now had In the basement. Will learned a lot about his parents, and mom learned that it was not always necessary to contradict her husband. She agreed whole-heartily with the advice he had given.

After a hearty dinner, Will called Lane. "Hi, have some time for a conversation this evening?... Yeah? Good... see you about nine?... great...bye."

"Well, folks, I'll be out of here at about eight fifteen. Lane says she has some news for me."

Mom looked alarmed, so Will assured her. "No, it's nothing to be alarmed about. Just news. Any last-minute things we haven't talked about?"

Dad took this one. "Nope." He put on some music and the three of them sat around listening.

At Lane's house, Will was welcomed with a huge hug. Lane led him to a couch and started talking. "Ever since you popped up in Amy's place, I've been talking to that school we went to about granting you a Bachelor's degree.

"Remember Mrs. Moss, the Literature teacher?" Will nodded. "I told her the story of your last semester, she checked with a bunch of people, and now there's a surprise waiting for you in her office. A couple surprises, in fact."

Will was intrigued. "What could it be, a B.A.?"

"Well, that's part of it. She actually contacted some of your classmates, you know, the ones you tutored. Then she looked at all your books. As the dean of the Liberal Arts Department, Dr. Moss granted you a Bachelor's in Education and a Master's in Creative Writing. She wants to talk to you about a teaching job."

Will looked at her, a little stunned. "Wow."

"So what did you want to talk about?"

"First thank you, and I'll thank Dr. Moss later. I wanted to check how you're doing, with the divorce concept."

"Oh that... I signed off on it electronically. The lawyer said it might take a couple weeks to clear and be public record, but to consider myself unattached."

"Sounds like you're not depressed."

Lane smiled. "No, nowhere near it."

"So I wondered if I should pursue a deeper relationship with you."

Lane took his hand. "My friend, as much as I love you it wouldn't work, a romance between us. The fact that one day was rather legendary could obscure the fact that we would tire of one another in about a year, tops. You're too damn smart, kind, polite and opinionated for me. Plus, you don't need me. From what Amy says, you need Harriet."

Will chuckled. "That obvious, huh?"

"Maybe not to you, but to the rest of the world. You're too honest to hide it. Go get her." Will kissed her cheek and left.

The next day, Will called the college. "Hi, Dr. Moss? Will MacLeish here... yes it has been... do you think you would have a few minutes for me today? I'm in the area... sure. Lunch is fine. I'll see you at noon, then... Lane told me how much you've done for me, and I want to thank you... Bye, see you in a little while."

Will's parents insisted on coming. Will thought that he would wind up being handed an envelope with two pieces of parchment. He was wrong.

Arriving at Dr. Moss' office at 11:40, Will was ready to have a 10-minute conversation about old times, pick up his degrees and leave. "William! Welcome back to campus. Mr. and Mrs. MacLeish, wonderful to see you again. We met at the annual Fall Fest, Will's last year here."

Peter shook her hand. "Yes we did. William introduced you as the best teacher on the campus. Seems he was right."

"Aah, the flattery. Hardly any time for that today, though. We have a ceremony and celebration lunch to get to."

Will balked. "Ceremony?"

"Just a small one. Half a dozen professors from the Arts College, in the Small Cafeteria. Don't be so shocked. Nothing happens around here without a ceremony, especially the recognition of such an accomplished alumnus."

In the Small Cafeteria, capacity 100 people, were a dozen Professors, Lane and a contingent of classmates from long ago, and about 100 students. Standing Room Only.

"Ladies and Gentlemen" Dr. Moss began "We are here to celebrate accomplishment, and dispense justice. Many years ago, William MacLeish attended this College, and after a distinguished three and a half years of top grades turned in incomplete work.

"We should have known that there was more to that story, but Mr. MacLeish disappeared before we could discover the truth. The truth was that he had spent too much time tutoring a dozen others so that they would graduate.

"Then, he went on to tremendous success as a writer. Today, I am very pleased to finally confer upon William MacLeish the Bachelor of Arts in Education." She draped the ribbon around his neck to hearty applause.

"And now, I introduce the Dean of Graduate Studies, Dr. Linus Severn."

Dr. Severn stepped up. "Thank you Dr. Moss. From the moment I read Thessalon, I knew that this writer was important. I knew that a mark was being made on the history of literature.

"The extent of that mark became obvious only recently, when Mr. MacLeish stepped out from behind his aliases.

"In recognition of his extraordinary work in the field of Creative Fiction, I hereby confer the Master of Arts degree, and well-earned it is, upon William MacLeish." Another ribbon, and a great deal more applause.

Dr. Moss resumed her position as Master of Ceremonies. "And now, we are proud to feed our astonished honoree, his parents, friends and classmates."

Those in the audience who were there to meet the author huddled around Will, trying to have even a moment of conversation and a handshake. Half an hour later, they seemed to fade out of the room.

Dr. Moss, Lane and classmates, and his parents filled a large circular table. Dr. Moss leaned over toward Will and quietly advised him "When Thessalon came out, some of the stories were familiar. Turns out, I recognized them from assignments. I keep your originals in a box next to the book, so I can appreciate the progression. Great fun."

Will grinned that his stories had been memorable. "Too bad it always happens electronically now. There are no earlier drafts sitting around. It would be interesting to see just how much my agent has done. He's my editor, too."

After some small talk and munching on what Will imagined was the best lunch a college cafeteria could possibly do, there were handshakes and broad smiles, and a few photographs.

On the way back to her car, Lane reminded Will "Don't forget, you told my class you would visit again. They've all turned in stories already."

"Oh, yeah..." He smiled mischievously. "How about tomorrow?"

Lane didn't blink an eye. "If you spend the rest of this afternoon at my place, you can read them all, and find things to comment on."

"Let's do that." Will called the folks, and got an invitation for Lane to come for dinner. When he finished reading the Elementary fiction, Will fell asleep on the couch. Forty-five minutes later, Lane woke him up.

"So what do you think?"

"Oh, ummm... I think that as fiction writers they threaten my career. Two in particular are about twenty years beyond their grade level. The rest are some of the best users of the language I've come across. I'm guessing that's all your fault."

Lane beamed. "That's right, friend. I'm that good at this teaching thing. By the way, we should leave soon for dinner with your folks."

"Oh, by the way..."

"What?"

"I didn't tell them."

"Didn't tell who what?"

"My parents. About my participation in Amy's arrival."

"Oh. This should be fun... do you not want them to know?"

"Not exactly that. I told them that you have a daughter, and that I got to spend some time with her."

"Just not that she's your daughter."

"I anticipate a disappointed tear in mom's eyes."

Lane punched his arm. "Men! You dipstick, the only disappointment would be not to know that they have a granddaughter, and what a gem she is."

Will seemed confused by that statement. "I'll let you leak that information. Mom's going to hit me with something anyway."

Will's parents were very interested in how Lane's life had been since college, and took a polite interest in pictures of her children. "Of course, William has not blessed us with grandchildren. I suppose there's still some hope." Looking at the picture of Amy, Will's mother squinted. "There's something familiar about her, maybe I've seen her around."

"Well, she grew up about ten miles away. You might have seen her. She's a lawyer now, one of the youngest ever. Smart as a whip. But I don't have to tell you about raising genius kids." Then Lane took the conversation a different direction. "She looks a bit like her father. She was born in March after graduation."

Mom looked at her. "There must be a story there."

Lane smiled. "There is indeed. It's a story I love, but have rarely told. The weekend before final exams of Senior year, I was having an anxiety attack. I was convinced that I was going to fail every test, that I hadn't learned anything.

"My parents had gone to a family wedding in Maine. A friend came to visit, to make sure I was okay. Anyway, this friend talked me down a bit, held my hand a while. I was calmer, but still worried. He put his arms around me and kissed me. I kissed him back, and that began some very nice and reassuring physical contact. Six hours later, I fell asleep.

"When I woke up, there was a note: 'Relax and ace your exams. You know everything you need to know.' This friend was one of the smartest people on campus, so I took his word for it. Sure enough, I got all high marks on the exams.

"Two months later, I figured out I was pregnant. Like they admit on the package, no contraceptive is 100% effective. Turns out, my affectionate friend had disappeared, nowhere to be found. I had just started dating a fellow I knew had been interested in me. When I told him, he asked me to marry him as soon as possible, so I did. He was an amazing father, and we had the two boys together."

As Lane was talking, Will's mother had sat next to her. "So who was this wandering Romeo?"

Lane just smiled. Mom went over and punched Will's arm.

"To be fair, he didn't know any of this until we met again recently."

"Can we meet her?"

"Thought you'd never ask. Your granddaughter is coming to my house for dinner next week. I know she wants to meet you, too." As far as Will's mom was concerned, Lane's invitation more than made up for Will's silence on the matter.

"Thank you."

....

The next morning, it was 8th grade again. "Good morning, young writers! So glad to see you all again! I've had a chance to read all your work, and I have to say that you are all terrific writers. If I had known how good you are, I would have designed a harder assignment.

"While all of you did very well, I would like to point out two pieces that were very interesting. These two authors took on challenges that most writers, even published ones, would not have.

"First is Mary Claire Sullivan. She has written an entire story as thoughts in the narrator's mind. Things the character sees and feels and thinks. This kind of storytelling is difficult because of the lack of dialog, but I would like to commend Mary for a successful piece of work.

"Second, and no less in quality, is Ali al-Fahd, with a story about being new in a place. In seven pages, he shows the isolation and the value of a welcoming smile.

"I think that it would be valuable for your whole school, and the high school too, to see what good work you are doing, and be inspired by it. With your permission, and if need be your parents' permission, I would like to have a small magazine printed with all of your stories in it."

The classroom exploded in cheers. Lane nodded. "I think we can arrange that. Maybe it's time our school had a literary magazine." More cheers.

After some more conversation (quieted by request of the class next door), Will was off. A hug and a peck on his cheek was witnessed by Lane's class, and she could imagine the musical "Whooooooh" that they held back.

11

By the time Will's hired car arrived at the Broome Street address it was 2 PM. No answer at the door, so he wandered in. There was a note on the table.

Will,

We went to Bob's at noon. Be back later.

Amy

Huh. All day at the Reverend's place. Will wondered what that was about. Will went to sleep on the couch, thinking to ask when he saw her.

At 1:00 in the morning, Amy burst in, laughing. Harvey stood over Will, slobbering all over the side of his head. Will woke up from all the fuss. "What's up?"

Amy's voice was distorted from smiling too wide. "Two things, just today. I was walking Harvey, and a woman stopped to admire him. We got to talking and stopped for coffee, and she has a law practice. I told her my story, and she asked me to come work with her, doing family law for women.

"Her office is a 5-minute walk away, and I can start any time. Probably part time at first.

"Then there's the huge news. Apparently, I'm engaged. Bob asked, I said yes. His bishop wants to meet me, but Bob says that's a formality."

Will was surprised. "Kinda quick, don'tcha think?"

Amy was still grinning, the light still in her eyes. "Sure, but Bob proposed a one-year engagement, so we can be sure, you know, that we even know one another."

"Cautious man. What the heck, congratulations. Hey, that brings up something I wanted to do anyway. Since you have work in the area, I want to give you this place. I think I want to spend my time in the country."

"Wow. I don't even know if I can pay the taxes and condo fees."

Will grinned. "There's an account for that. You get a checkbook with half a million in it, escrow for taxes and fees."

Amy, still grinning, asked "And when I get married?"

"You can use it for your office, a getaway, or sell it."

"God, Will. That's a lot to give somebody."

"It's nothing compared to getting the life I want. If it keeps that smile on your face, that's repayment enough."

Amy hugged him. "Thank you. Now dry off and go back to sleep."

In the morning, Will called Seamus. "Hi, guy, it's your favorite author...no, the other one... can you put the condo in Amy's name and the house in Harriet's?... oh... how about co-owners?... right... oh... let's go with the transfers.... Yeah, I know it's crazy... thanks, man. I'll send you a bonus... hahahaha...okay, do it for free."

When the van pulled up to his house in the country, Will's driver for the day called out "Here you are, Mister M... home at last!"

Will and Harvey had fallen asleep in the back. Harvey woke up faster at the word 'home', and found it necessary to run out and reclaim his kingdom. Will opened the door, and Harvey jumped across his lap and went running. "Thank you. Such a smooth ride it's like being in the ultimate soft bed with a white noise machine."

"That's what you paid for, glad you're satisfied."

Will tried to give the driver a tip. "No thanks, sir... the boss pays me quite enough."

Will was insistent. "But you have the whole trip home to do."

"Mister MacLeish, I live for the long drive home. I don't have to be there for another four hours, since we made good time on our way here, so I can stop for anything I want, take it easy. You have a good time out here in the country." The driver lugged the luggage out of the back. "I can take it into the house.."

"No thanks. I'll get that." Will shook the man's hand, and the van pulled away. While they had been talking, Harvey had found a new person on his porch, and already made a new friend.

Will walked up to the stairs to the porch. "Hi, I'm..."

The woman petting Harvey interrupted. "William MacLeish, famous author, whose house this is." She stood. "And I am Maria, Harriet's mother." She went to shake Will's hand. "So what exactly are your intentions toward my daughter? Have a seat, and let's talk."

Will took a seat. It had been a long time since he was interviewed by a parent. "As far as my intention, I want to be the good man in the lives of your daughter and her sons. I think having the right man in the mix makes things easier. Looking into the future, I would like to marry her, and I would be delighted if we had a child together."

Maria grinned. "Okay, so you're a writer. You are very well spoken. What would it take for you to hit her, or the boys?"

Will blinked at the thought. "There is no excuse anyone could make for such an action. I have never hit a woman or a minor, and the only time I hit anyone was to protect a third person."

"Tell me."

"I was with some acquaintances, hiking. One of the smaller, thinner guys was being an idiot. He aggravated a bigger guy, somebody I knew from High school, until he was about to really hurt the smaller guy. As he drew back his fist, I punched the big one in the shoulder hard enough to leave a bruise. I told the big guy that it wasn't worth putting the little guy in the hospital. The whole group agreed that the little guy should either apologize and behave or leave. He left, and the rest of the hike went smooth and peaceful."

Maria looked at him, trying to decide the truth of the story. "Assuming all of that is true, and I believe that your dog supports it, we should make a plan. Harriet is very wary of quick marriages. Her first, she knew him three months and he died in a gang war. She had thought he was a good guy, not a gang member.

"So don't talk to her of marriage for now. Tell her you want to be around her and the boys. Live with us. Let her get more comfortable. Then, a few months down the road tell her you'd like to make it official. Meanwhile, just be nice. Not overly, but pleasant and helpful."

Will understood. "So I shouldn't put the house in her name yet>"

Maria giggled. "The thought that you thought to do that tickles me, but no, not yet. Just be her guy. She already likes you. Lucky she hasn't found another place yet."

Will understood. "Okay then, that's the plan. I'll be the boyfriend for as long as I can manage, then casually mention that I would like us to be married. I'll talk to her about living together when she gets home from work."

Maria nodded. "She might stay late. She really likes the work, and the people there. Thanks for arranging that."

"All I did was introduce her to someone I knew who was looking for an employee. Glad it worked out." They sat there satisfied for a while, future in-laws enjoying the landscape from the front porch.

The boys got home first. They recognized Will from some distance and ran to the porch. "Mister MacLeish! Thanks for letting us use your house, the place is beautiful!! There's so much space between things out here, it's amazing. Hi, grandma."

Will smiled at them. "Glad you're enjoying it. School okay? Other students?"

The boys took turns answering. "School's great, and most of the other kids too, plus we get to use the library, the computers and the gym."

They looked at one another. "Mister MacLeish, do you fish?"

"Sure. Do you?" Will was surprised.

"Actually, some of the guys invited us to come with them, but all we know is to throw the lure in the water and hope. The way they talk about things, there's a lot more to it."

"And when is this invitation for?"

"They go out Saturday mornings, early."

"Well, that doesn't give us a lot of time. You're right, there is more to it, with the small streams and ponds around here. I'll ask your mom, and see if we can get started tomorrow afternoon."

The boys let out a unanimous "Yay!" and ran off to their room.

"You're sure making points with them." Maria noted.

"Well heck, I've been out here more than twenty years, fishing spring, summer and fall, so I guess I can spare the time to show them a few things. People always took time with me when I was younger, so it makes sense to pass it on."

Eventually, Harriet pulled into the driveway. Will had thought to hide and surprise her, but thought better of it. When the car pulled in, Maria quietly went inside.

Harriet grinned to see Will sitting on the porch. "Well if it isn't the landlord! How was Scotland?" She kissed him for a minute.

"Beautiful, and lonely. There was no you."

"Good answer. Are you here to kick us out?"

"No, I'm here to join the group, if that's alright. Think you could bear to live with me? Romantically speaking, of course."

Harriet acted like she was thinking about it. "Depends. Do you do windows?"

"Every six months, like clockwork."

"Well then I suppose... on a trial basis, of course."

"Of course."

Giggles, high fives and dancing were heard from inside the house.

Will thought of the other question he wanted to ask. "Okay with you if I take the boys fishing tomorrow afternoon? Probably about two hours at a local creek."

Harriet was a little hesitant. Not that she didn't trust Will, but these were her babies they were talking about. "Well..."

Will had the answer to the question she wasn't asking. "I plan to get them each a walkie-talkie like the one I carry when I go fishing. Around here it's more dependable than cell phones when you're out in the woods. I've used mine at distances up to twenty-five miles. Gives them immediate access to the base station in the house or one another. It'll only take a couple minutes to show you how that works."

Harriet was impressed. "Sounds like you've thought this through."

"When I'm fishing alone, I turn to the channel for one of my friends up here. Help can arrive in a few minutes. And they'll be with me, so there won't be any emergencies."

"Okay, up to two and a half hours, I'm assuming not far away."

"Three miles down the road, and a five minute walk on a hiking trail. I'll make a map." Will thought he was starting to sound like a kid himself, pleading for this.

"Okay, you boys can go fishing. If you all come back unharmed, you can do it again sometime" Harriet took his arm and they walked into the house to tell everyone.

Dinner was fun. Maria made Arroz con Pollo, and Will introduced the family to baked apples with cheesy stuffing. Afterward, Will showed everyone how the walkie-talkies and base unit worked. The boys were especially excited. When the boys were advised about the new household arrangement with Will moving in, they grinned. "Told ya that first day! We were right!" Harriet blushed a little that her sons not only understood but had assessed Will's character faster than she had.

When the boys went up to bed, Harriet and Will sat on the couch, talking. Harriet started. "I keep thinking I should slow down or speed up, as far as really deeply trusting you. Don't know what to do.

Will, as usual, had an opinion. "Maybe trust me about one thing at a time. Trust me not to lie to you. If I say something, I mean it. You've agreed to trust me with your children, that's a big thing. You can trust me to cook for you.

"I will never demand anything of you. I am on your side. Anything that makes you more comfortable, just let me know."

Harriet looked at him. "Who built you? I would like to meet your parents."

Will chuckled to himself. "They want to meet you too. They think you might be an illusion." Harriet kissed him. That led to more kissing. Maria came into the room, gave them a minute, and said "Get a room, you two. I want to watch TV." They were off in a flash.

Maria decided that it was a perfect decision to give Harriet the master bedroom, and take the adjacent one for herself. Harriet was known to make noise occasionally.

....

The next day, Jorge and Miguel came running to the house at 3:00. Will was waiting on the porch. "Hey, guys. First, we have orientation. You'll want to not wear your good shoes, there's mud where we're going. Change out of anything you don't want to get dirty." They thundered up the stairs with a "Hi grandma, we're home!", then down again just as loudly. Once they were back, Will began his schpeel.

"You each get one of these backpacks, and a rod and reel. In the pack is a first aid kit, a clear box with lures, and a walkie-talkie. That last thing is for emergencies only. Real emergencies. To use it, you pick it up, turn it on, and say 'Breaker Breaker, TR2201 do you read?'. Both of you, and the base station and I are on the same channel. Once someone answers, you can talk back and forth."

Once they understood how the walkie-talkies worked, Will moved on to the fishing gear. A few minutes of casting practice and they took off in Will's car. The boys had been so focused on fishing that they had not noticed it in the driveway.

"Sweet wheels!"

"Yeah, it's a classic. Gets me where I want to go, and fits what I want to take with me."

....

They returned from fishing right on schedule, two and a half hours later. Will pulled into the garage, and tried to sneak in the back door. Maria noticed his bare feet. "Que pasa?"

"Harriet in?"

"No, about half an hour."

"We found a little mud. Thought I'd take care of it before she got home."

Maria smiled. "Men and mud. Can't stay away from one another. Go on, then. I know nothing."

Will kissed her cheek, and ran upstairs. When he came back down, he was carrying two better pairs of shoes and socks to match. "The boys are hosing off the shoes and socks they wore, and the ankles of their jeans. Maybe some paper towels would help." Maria waved a hand at him as he nabbed a roll.

When Harriet did get home, there were three people fishing in the side yard. "Catching anything? Crickets, maybe?"

Jorge ran to her. "Mom! Welcome home! We all caught fish, all different kinds. Mister MacLeish knows all about fishing, and he showed us a lot today. It was great!"

Harriet looked at Will, trying to figure out what her son wasn't telling her. Miguel filled in. "And we saw a deer, a couple snakes and a raccoon and all kinds of birds we never saw before!"

Will recognized the suspicion in her eyes. "And we found some mud, so we cleaned up before you got home. We had a great time, hope we can do it again."

Harriet kissed him. "Guess it's like mama says, 'boys and mud, can't keep them apart.' As long as I don't have to clean up after, have all the fun you want."

The next morning after Harriet and the kids left for their days, Maria continued with her now-favorite project: reading all of Will's books. Will dove into his overly complex story, which he supposed would take a couple years to complete. He forgot about lunch, and suddenly it was four o'clock. The boys were back. He heard them playing with Harvey, running circles around the house.

The barking stopped, and Will presumed that they were taking a break, all piled up in a happy lump on the lawn. The alarm in Jorge's voice erased that image. "Mister MacLeish! Mister MacLeish! Something's wrong!"

Will ran outside. He saw Jorge and Manuel, but no Harvey. "What's up?"

"It's Harvey. We were playing, then he stood still, sniffed the air, and took off running. Running real fast."

Will considered the possibilities. "Which way did he go?"

Manuel pointed to one of the paths through the woods. Will took out his phone and dialed. "Hi Jane... where is Marisa?... it's the white one with the big porch, on Cold Road, right?...okay, call the police and meet me there. Harvey just went running that direction." Will had only seen Harvey take off like that twice. Both times, Marisa had been in trouble.

With a word to Maria, Will took off, driving as fast as he safely could toward Mace's grandmother's house. When he pulled in, he was just in time to see Harvey ram his big head through a panel of the front door. A menacing bark and a couple gunshots followed. Will charged in after his friend.

The first thing Will saw was Mace on the floor, a gun in his hand, bleeding from his neck, wrist and leg. Harvey's fangs were still clenched at his neck. Both of them were bleeding and unconscious. Then Will heard crying from another corner of the room. Marisa was huddled there shaking, trying to make herself smaller, staring at Mace and Harvey.

Will went over to her. "It's over. You're safe. Come on, let's get you out of here." Marisa was in shock, and didn't walk when Will lifted her, so he carried her outside to his car. Moments later, Jane and the police car arrived. Jane went straight to her daughter.

Will was glad to see Don Herter, the village Chief of Police who happened to be on duty. "What happened?" Will led him inside. The chief looked around, thought about what he saw, and narrated.

"Bullet holes over in the corner, I guess Mace was shooting. Was Marisa over there in the corner?"

Will nodded. "Running away from Mace."

"Right. Then Harvey comes through the door, sees her in danger, and attacks. Mace shoots Harvey, but too late."

Will commented "I heard two or three shots, then nothing."

"So what brought you here, Will?"

"Harvey was playing with the kids in the yard, and he suddenly took off running. The path he took pretty much leads here. Harvey would do that, know when she was in trouble and take off running to save her."

"Yeah. Jane told me about him saving her in High School. I better see if Marisa can tell us anything." He went over to the car, and Will went back inside.

Will sat next to Harvey, petting his head. "You did it, bud. You saved her again. Saved her life. Now you can relax, she's safe. I love you, Harvey." Will would later discount the idea that Harvey's whole body relaxed at that moment merely because he had died. Will knew that this was love. Harvey had taught him all about it.

Outside at Jane's car, Don was trying to coax a few words out of Marisa. Will came up close to her and gently said "Marisa, look at me. Look for the truth in my eyes. You're safe. I guarantee it. Harvey made sure of it. We need you to tell us what happened."

Marisa looked at him and tears streamed down her face. "He went out... for supplies... we were cleaning... having a good time... he came back crazy, saying I wanted to trap him... that I was evil... I put out my hand to calm him down and he hit my hand... punched me... said he would shoot me... but he hated guns... he started shooting... I ran... he cornered me... walking toward me... Harvey came in, grabbed his hand... he dropped the gun, picked it up with his other hand... Harvey bit his leg... Mace pointed the gun at Harvey... Harvey went for his neck... Mace shot then fell over, Harvey still with him... then you came in."

Will wrapped his arms around her. "Thank you. We all needed to know."

After a moment, Marisa asked "Harvey died protecting me, didn't he?" Will nodded. Marisa, calmer, noted "Mace was the one person Harvey never warmed up to. I thought he was jealous of the attention I gave Mace. God, was I wrong."

Don had something to say. "I don't think this was about Mace. I knew him pretty well. There's been a few incidents involving Angel Dust recently; I think this is one of them. I think somebody spiked Mace's food or drink. We'll do everything we can to find out who. Do you know exactly where he was going?"

Marisa nodded. "Yeah. Hardware store, then 7-11 on the way back. We both liked Lemon Slurpees and Moon Pies."

"Thank you. I'll take a close look."

"You mean it wasn't his fault?"

Don smiled, and adjusted his equipment belt. "Mace hated drugs. He was helping the school with an anti-drug campaign for this coming school year. I guarantee it wasn't Mace who did this. It was the drug."

Will addressed her again. "You need anything?"

Marisa shook her head. "Maybe just to go home and cry." Jane secured her daughter's seat belt and pulled out slowly.

Will walked over to the Sheriff. "So what do you think?"

"I think somebody in the drug trade didn't want Mace around and gave him too much and handed him a gun. Somebody he trusted. If he was going to the hardware store and the 7-11, I need to stake out the 7-11, look for people he was in school with, maybe. Sorry about Harvey, but we could have shot Mace several times without stopping him, and he still had five rounds in the gun. Marisa would be dead."

Will kicked the gravel of the driveway. "Yeah. I'll be home if you need me."

"Oh, Will… congratulations on the girlfriend. I met her when I went for an oil change on my truck. Maybe this time you get lucky and it's permanent?"

Will smiled. "Yeah, maybe."

At the house, Will told the group what had happened. Jorge and Manuel volunteered that they had seen a couple sleazy guys around the high school, and they'd keep an eye out. Will hid in the study with a large brandy.

Will's phone rang. "Oh, hi Jane... yeah... oh, that's good... how are you doing?... right... hey thanks for calling." Somehow, knowing that Marisa was safe at home and sedated for the overnight made Will feel better.

At dinner, Harriet expressed the group's sentiment. "Sorry about Harvey. Anything we can do?"

Will smiled at the thought. "Nothing necessary. He was really old. I always thought he'd lay down for a nap one of these days and not wake up. He was a great dog, a great friend, and even a better Christian than I have been."

Harriet needed that last one explained. "A better Christian?"

"Yeah. Remember the story from the Bible in which some of the Jewish religious lawyers challenged Christ 'Tell us the Law?' And at the time, there were libraries of volumes of Jewish law. Remember what Christ said?"

"Sure. 'Love one another'."

"Well Harvey did a better job of loving everybody he met than I ever did. I just try to follow the example. So guys, what's the plan on this fishing trip?"

Manuel responded "Oh, they cancelled. Maybe another time."

"Gosh, that's too bad, but it opens up another possibility. I was thinking earlier, about Harvey. He used to love to wander back in the woods behind the house. That made me remember something. When I bought the house, I had a chance to own a lot of property back there.

"I had forgotten, when I forgot some other things, that I actually own the woods. The local Nature Conservancy arranged that as long as it's left wild and I take care of it, I don't pay property taxes on 200 acres, with its own stream. We have our own fishing spot. It's one of the cleanest streams in the county. Want to go there Saturday?"

The boys responded with an excited "Yeah!"

Will looked at Harriet. "It's a mile straight back behind the house, and nobody else goes there. We'd be out of your hair all morning."

Harriet was amused. "Looks like you three are starting a club. Sure, you can go as long as the students finish their work."

After dinner, Will and Harriet cleared the dishes and cleaned everything. Will had a thought. "I... I mean we can get a dishwasher, you know."

"Don't you dare! I love washing dishes, and having nice dishes to wash. It's a quiet thing to do with somebody. Once in a while, washing dishes with the boys they'll tell me something I didn't know, or something they're thinking about. A dishwasher would take that away."

Will appreciated the perspective. "Then we won't do that.." He kissed her and went back to rinsing and drying.

Later, playing a game with Manuel and Jorge, Will had an observation. "Hey, this is a happy part of your life, right?"

Both the boys nodded, their concentration on the game. "Well who do you think makes it that way?"

Shrugs.

"Your mom and grandmom. All the cooking, cleaning, your mom taking on a hard job, that's all so your life gets better."

Manuel: "So?"

"You could say thanks once in a while. Tell them you love them, too."

Jorge: "Mushy."

Will had a solution for that problem. "So maybe there's something you could do instead of say. You've heard the saying 'Actions speak louder that words'. They gave up all their friends and stuff in NYC so you'd be safe, because they love you. I figure that earns them a little something once in a while."

Both boys stopped playing.

"When you do something for someone else, do they say thank you?"

Nodding.

"I'm just saying, once in a while, maybe at random, say thanks, give some love back." Will made a few more moves in the game while they were thinking. "Boo yah! I win!"

"Cheater." The boys went off, but he had planted a seed in their minds. He couldn't wait to see what developed.

The next day he heard about it. The boys came home exuberant "The teacher said we're all caught up to where the kids we'll be in class with are! We don't have to go to school until September 4th!" They put their school things in their room and came back down. "Hey, Grandma... anything we can do to make your day easier?"

Will heard, and smiled. When Harriet arrived and heard, she went straight to him. "Alright... what did you do to my wonderful but normally work-avoiding sons?"

"Whatever could you mean? Did something happen with the boys?"

"You could say that. On their way from school, they stopped at work, brought me some ice cream, and asked if I needed any help. They actually wanted to do something. Then on their way out, they yelled 'Love ya, mom!'. Now either you did something to them, they want something, or I don't know what. Tell me they aren't broken."

Without looking up, Will intoned "Seem okay to me... last I heard they were doing something for your mom." Harriet ran into the house. A few minutes later she came back out, looking dazed.

"They're dusting the upstairs hall and the stairs, then they're going to help make dinner. Oh God, my teens are warped. Maybe it's all this fresh air... it's getting them stoned."

This time Will looked up. "Nothing to worry about. Sounds like somebody introduced them to the concept of gratitude, and they finally realized how much they have to be grateful for. They'll probably settle down, like teens do with a new idea. Then they'll be pleasantly helpful, grateful and expressive." Harriet seemed to buy it, for the moment.

A week and a half later, with Will starting to get used to his new family life, Harriet came home worried. "Why don't we argue about anything? It's not normal."

Will was too relaxed to worry. "Maybe because we agree on things. I hear that happens sometimes."

"On everything?"

"Maybe the fact that you've discovered my basic sanity and good-guy status, and I think you're a marvelous human being has something to do with it."

"Marvelous? Okay. Don't you think you've been seduced into your current situation?"

Will chuckled. "Seduced into something I've dreamed of all my life? What's to protest? Only one thing left to make this the dream."

"Oh yeah, that. A little more time."

"Sure, no pressure. I'm not going anywhere."

Harriet sat on his lap, kissing him. "Somehow, I actually believe that."

12

Talking to Morris, Will brought up one of his idle curiosities. "Hey, should I get a gun? Don't want to miss out on the culture of the countryside, if something's the norm."

Morris' turn to chuckle. "Twenty some years you've lived here. You ever need a gun?"

"Sure. The year of the coyotes. If Harvey hadn't chased them off, they would have come in to raid the fridge."

"Yeah, but that's a couple months out of all that time. Would it have been worth twenty years of target practice and training, or only a phone call? You could have called, and any one of a dozen guys would have come and either chased them off or buried them, your choice."

"Phone call is cheaper, I suppose."

"Yeah. Plus the kids can't shoot themselves with it."

Will was a little disappointed. "Seems like a manly thing."

"Hell, Will, don't fall for that macho junk. Around here, a guy only buys the tools he needs."

"Okay, what do I need for a home invasion? Now that the whole world knows who I am, I figure somebody's going to get the bright idea to come get some stuff."

Morris had to think about that. "So that's scenario one. Crooks are usually smart enough to wait 'til everybody's out of the house, in which case there's nothing to do about it.

"Scenario two, where there's somebody in the house is a problem. Whatever thing you choose to defend your stuff with, every member of the household has to be able to use it safely.

"Scenario three, you get kidnapped. That one gets touchy. Involve the police or don't, pay the ransom or don't, and rely on the kidnappers to release you, or don't.

"In all three, a gun is not your best bet. Something small that you have with you at all times would be some help, unless the kidnappers find it and laugh. Something like a multi-tool might help, but they're nearly impossible to conceal.

"In any case, a gun is likely not to help. Get some pepper spray, something like that. Might give you a better chance to get away from whatever situation. Some of those come in a pen size.

"So my advice to you is that unless you're taking up hunting or target shooting, which you are welcome to do, don't get a gun. If you do take up hunting, get all the training available, and the tool that does the job. Just so happens I have three. A .22 that I bought when I was sixteen and use for small varmints, a .270 that was a gift from my father so we could go together during deer season, and a shotgun that I got to go duck hunting but found out I don't really like duck hunting so I use it to chase away crows and starlings. I load it with salt and fertilizer pellets so there's not a lot of lead in the ground."

Will absorbed all that. "That might be the longest string of words I've ever heard fall out of your mouth. You get around to talking pretty good after a couple beers. I take it that you think I shouldn't get a gun."

"Yup. You should get another dog as soon as you're ready. Protection, companionship and undying loyalty all in one package. And at the shelter they cost way less than a gun."

Will went home to think.

Another evening, Harriet mumbled another issue. "I'm getting suspicious about you again."

"About what?"

"You're all too comfortable with all of us invading your house. I think you've had a full house before."

Will was surprised. "Nope. Never more than one person at a time. Don't mistake my comfort with you, Maria and the boys for comfort with people in general. This number of other people in the house would constitute the building limit, and only acceptable for about two hours at a time. I guess it's love." He got an awfully big kiss for that.

Another day, some of what Morris had said started to sink in. Defending himself and defending the house and occupants could most probably be done without a gun. But there was something coming up that might require one. Will's book tour would be a different situation. Out in public, some of the fans could be crazed... Will started to get worried. He decided to call an expert.

"Hi, agent Pollack, please... Will MacLeish calling... Hi, Tim. Would you have some time to advise me? I've got a national book tour coming up, and personal safety is... right... right... Oh that would be great. Day after tomorrow? I can do that. I'll send you the list of planned events, but there might be more by the time the tour starts. See you then."

Cool. Advice from the FBI. Tim had been a valuable reference for a couple of books, and Will trusted him. He could provide information and strategies to keep a guy safe.

At dinner, Will let everyone know that he would be away for the day. "Research for this new book. I'm going to D.C. to interview a specialist in corruption. Unfortunately, I'll be gone all day, getting back late."

Manuel was excited. "Washington D.C.? Can we come?"

Will grinned at the enthusiasm. "Not this time, it's all work. We could arrange a visit for us, though. Maybe a long weekend, with a tour guide and a nice hotel. I understand now is a good time to visit."

Manuel thought this was a great idea. "Can we bring mom and granma?"

"Of course. I bet your mom's boss would give her a day off, if we asked nicely."

Harriet yielded to the family pressure evident in her son's eyes and her mother's smile. "Sure. We can do that."

....

Three days later, Morris came over to see Will, all excited. "Will! There's an opportunity! I know you've resisted coming hunting with us, but somebody should take advantage of this!"

Will looked at him, trying to think of what kind of tranquilizer to recommend. "What's the hubbub, bub?"

"Oh man... Mrs. Oderheim is selling her husband's gun collection. He died a couple years ago, and she just got into the gun safe. Will, there's a mint condition Henry 30-30 she'll let go for $100."

"So?"

Morris was frustrated. "So if you tried to buy this thing new, it would be $1000! This is the kind of rifle that gets handed down for generations. If you ever considered hunting in all these years I've been inviting you, this is the deer rifle you would want to use."

"Why?"

Morris slumped down. "You ever see a cowboy movie?"

"Sure."

"Well, did you notice the rifle a lot of people carried?"

"Sure. The one with the loop behind the trigger, to cock it. Like that TV show 'The Rifleman'".

Encouraged, Morris continued. "The better one of those is a Henry. The Henry company invented them in 1860. By the end of the Civil War, every soldier who could afford one was using a Henry. The company still makes them."

"Huh. I thought that was Winchester."

"Winchester got a license to manufacture from Henry."

"Cool. So why does all this want to make me hunt deer?"

"If you really don't want to, that's fine. If you think you would ever want to hunt, or even take up target shooting, you could buy it now and use it later. Will, even used and beat up, they go for $500. You could leave it in my safe."

Twenty years of a close friendship is worth a lot of trust. "Okay, Morris. Since you think it's such a good idea, let's do it.?"

"So what's the process?"

"We all go to the gun store. She has to turn it over, sort of sell it to the store. They check if it's been stolen or used in a crime, then they sell it to you. The check usually takes a couple days."

Morris' enthusiasm was starting to infect Will. On the way to the gun store to meet Mrs. Oderheim, Will asked "So I know nothing about guns. Where do I learn? From you?"

"Nah. The guys at the range can get you a certificate that you know your way around your gun. Shooting, cleaning, maintenance, everything."

"Good."

Arriving at Trace's Gun Shop, the friends saw Mrs. Oderheim struggling with a box. Morris rushed over. "Here, let me help you." The box was a wood presentation case.

When the group went inside, owner's eyes widened. "You're kidding." He took the case and opened it. "Wow. Looks like mint condition. And here's the sales receipt... 1940. Wow."

Mrs. Oberheim filled in a little history. "Claus' father bought it when Germany invaded Poland. He was afraid that the Germans would invade us. He never did wind up using it. Claus hunted with it once or twice, but liked a different rifle he had better. He maybe used a whole box of shells."

Trace made sure there weren't any bullets in the rifle, and put a camera down the muzzle. "Yup, mint condition." With that receipt, and knowing the history, I can clear this weapon overnight. Just have to fire it once and send the bullet to the lab for the crime report."

Morris was itchy to get this done. "So we come back tomorrow?"

"Sure. I do need fingerprints of the buyer, and photo ID."

Will stepped up. "That's me…"

Mrs. Oderheim touched his arm. "I have very much enjoyed your books. I hope you get some good use from this old thing."

Will kissed her hand. "I will. I have a novel coming out soon. I'll bring your signed copy over as soon as it's available."

Will had never seen a 90-year-old woman giggle like a 16-year-old. It was heartwarming. "Thank you, Mister MacLeish. I know I will greatly enjoy that."

On the way home, Will gave Morris a thought. "This doesn't mean I'll ever go hunting, but I appreciate you letting me know about the availability. When I was a teen, I went to summer camp, and they had a shooting range. Just air pistols and BB guns. That was kind of fun. Most likely I'll do target shooting."

Morris was satisfied. "Cool. Going to keep it in my vault?"

"Yeah. That's free, right?"

"Cost you one dinner a year."

"Deal."

Later, Will told Harriet that he had bought a gun. She started yelling. "No, no. It can't come in the house, I'll leave you over this! I thought you were a nice guy! Damnit!"

Once she stopped, Will quietly explained that the rifle would live at Morris' house, in a vault, and only come out so he could learn everything about it, and maybe do some target shooting or go hunting with Morris. The gun would not be anywhere unsafe.

"Swear it. Swear it on your life."

Will held up his right hand. "I swear it on my life. No gun or ammunition in the house. Ever."

Harriet still pouted. "Okay then. And you won't promote guns to the boys."

"No, I won't. Once they're of legal age to own one, I will answer any questions they have."

"I suppose that's fair. I should have known you'd never endanger the boys, I think protecting them is part of what you'll do. It's just that guns are part of the problem where we used to live."

Will put his arm around her. "Yeah. Here, they're a tool, to keep the crops safe. Morris says they donate most of the deer to the Rome Homeless shelter. They sell the hide and bones and antlers, and use the meat that gets cleared by the health authorities to feed people. I won't necessarily do any hunting, but it seems like at least Morris does it responsibly, safely."

"Yeah, I like Morris. Jane too. Just be very careful. Those things go off when you least expect."

Will kissed her. "I promise I won't get hurt or die from the gun, or anybody else's either. Aquarius doesn't die from violence, because they can see it coming. We trip over things and fall into manholes because we're too focused on what's farther ahead."

A week later, a call came from the hospital. From what Will could gather, Manuel and Jorge were there, being treated for some non-critical injuries. The hospital needed a family member to pick them up when they were discharged.

Not knowing why nobody had called to say the boys were hurt, Will let Maria know he was going out and drove downtown to get Harriet.

"What do you mean, they're in the hospital? How'd they get there? How hurt are they? Oh my God, now I have to pay a hospital on top of worrying about my sons..."

Will was not as panicked. "You don't get to pay a bill. Thought I had told you: I put all four of you on my health insurance the day you moved up here."

Harriet looked at him, stunned. "You what?"

"Put you on my insurance. I figured your insurance from work would lapse, and I wanted to make sure everybody was covered."

"You did that with no promises, no expectation of a relationship even. Just to make sure we were okay."

"Yeah."

Harriet stared at him for another minute. "Will..."

"Yes?"

"You remember that question you wanted to ask?"

"The big one?"

"That's it. The answer is yes."

Will stopped the car and parked on some gravel beside the two-lane road. "You sure?"

Harriet was crying. "I was sure at the picnic in the park, that first day. Now I can't resist what I want any longer." They spent a few minutes holding one another. Will realized why he had wanted a bench seat.

Once they both calmed down a little, Harriet remembered where they had been going. "We should go claim the kids. Oh gosh, how do we tell them?"

"Straight out. I proposed and you accepted. Your ring is back at the house."

At the hospital, the boys had a simple explanation. "We were walking around with the other guys and part of the trail gave way, and we fell through some bushes and onto some rocks."

Knowing the hiking possibilities nearby, Will asked "Where were you walking around?"

Jorge volunteered "From behind the school, headed toward town, then we turned back. Sort of a loop."

The doctor came in before Will could ask another question. "Hi Will, and you must be Ms. Meron... your sons described you perfectly. You'll be glad to know that these young men are not seriously hurt.

"They had scratches from raspberry bushes, some of which bled a drop or two. Must have looked dramatic to the older kids who drove them here. We cleaned all their scratches, and Jorge had a cut from a sharp rock that required one stitch.

"That's consistent with falling through some raspberry bushes into a dry stream bed. They'll both be fine in a couple days. Jorge can come back here or your family physician can take the stitch out in a few days."

On the way home, Will wondered who pushed them down what hill, and if they would ever tell. Arriving at the house, Will made some iced tea for everyone, then nodded at Harriet.

"Boys..." Harriet's voice shook a little. "There's some news. Mister MacLeish asked me to marry him and I said yes."

Jorge and Manuel grinned at one another, did a high five. "About time! We've been waiting for that. The only questions are 1) 'Do we call him dad, or Mister M, or what?' and 2) Do we keep our last name or take MacLeish?"

Will answered that. "How about calling me Will, like everybody else? And I'm thinking that you can choose whether to use my last name or the one you already have. Your mom and I haven't nailed down all the details yet."

Jorge hugged Will and then his mother. "Cool. Congratulations, both of you. Hope it lasts forever. Think I'll lay down for a while."

Manuel had pretty much the same reaction. "Yeah, cool. Lot of excitement today. Think I'll lay down too."

Once they were out of the room, Harriet asked "Any idea what they're hiding?"

Will had an idea. "Maybe who pushed them and how sore they feel. Blackberry thorns are torture."

"Think it's anything to worry about?"

"Probably not, but let's keep an eye out. So it's an interesting question for you, too. Do you want to keep your current last name or share mine?" Will could feel that the answer might not come quickly.

....

When Will picked up the rifle, he took it to the range. He signed up for the Use and Maintenance 2-day course, and continuing target training. Two or three days a week should do it. He was right. The owners, Freddy and Zeke, were full of information, advice and tips. Turns out, they spent long stretches of time, like any retailer does, with nobody in the store. The two of them appreciated anyone who would listen. Will became close to both of them rather quickly.

After a month he was regularly hitting bulls-eyes at 100 yards. The success made the activity more enjoyable, once he got the right earplugs.

Often, Will and Morris would go shooting together. Once they found a time with the fewest other shooters, they took advantage and would have the 12-station range either to themselves or with one other person. On one such day, Morris had finished off a box of ammunition, and gone inside to clean his gun. Zeke, the owner sounded a buzzer in each station. Over the PA system, the warning came "Cease fire, cease fire. Maintenance is on the range."

As was normal, Will put down his gun. Zeke was going out to get Morris' target. As Zeke wandered out across the range, Will heard a snarl and snort from the left side of the range.

What's that, a bear? No, a pig. Pig the size of a bear oh god it's running at Zeke. Can't let that happen. Distract the pig. One to the butt. Aim, pull the trigger. Oh good, it's looking this way. Step out from the shooting station and yell SOOOEE SOOOOEE! OVER HERE! HA PIG! Well that worked. Cock the gun, aim, pull the trigger. Still running this way, cock the gun, aim, pull the trigger. Still running, did I miss? Cock the gun, aim, pull the trigger. Still moving, a pig that size can and will kill a man cock the gun, aim, pull the trigger. It stopped running. Just standing there. Collapsing. Somebody next to me aiming an assault rifle. It's over. Dead pig on the range.

More talking, somebody hugging. Walk over to the carcass. The dead thing. The thing that was running around before it was shot and killed. The thing that maybe had a life, a family, a favorite thing to eat. Before I killed it. Rifle still in right hand, finger on the trigger in case it moves. No movement. I'm sorry Mister Pig, I truly am. You seemed very angry, and were running at Zeke like you wanted to kill something. I had to stop you. I had to.

Zeke came over to where Will was sitting, five feet away from the boar. The way Will was staring at the carcass, Zeke knew the man was in shock. After all, a target shooter kills at least three hundred pounds of wild boar, it has to be a surprise. A shock to the system. "Come on, Will. Let's get you out of here. You saved my life, man. You did it. Here, I'll carry the Henry. I'll clean it for you, while you relax a minute. Come on inside."

Will was a zombie for the ride home, silent, staring straight ahead. As he stopped the car in Will's driveway, Morris asked "Hey, Will... you going to be alright?"

Will took a deep breath. "Yeah. Of course. Where did that come from?"

"What, the pig? One of the guys said there's a private hunting reserve..."

"No, the thing in me that kills without hesitation."

"You had to, Will. There was nobody else out there. By the time Freddy got onto the range with a gun, he only got to see it collapse. You saved Zeke from being mauled. Anything less than dead, that was a dangerous creature.

"Might have been able to disable it..."

"No. Not an option. Another few yards it would have killed you. And you know Harriet would have to blame me."

Will chuckled. "This whole thing was your idea, after all. Let's not tell her what happened."

"Deal."

13

After two days of Will's silence and staring out windows, Harriet demanded an explanation. "Alright, you. This is it. I know something is wrong, and you are going to tell me what it is."

Will took a deep breath, and told her the story. "I saw the life go out of that animal, because of what I did. I never want to see that again. Every time I close my eyes, I see it running toward Zeke or laying there dead. I know I did it to save Zeke, but this creature is still dead. It bothers me that I would do it again."

Harriet hugged him tight. "This only bothers you because you're such a good man. You don't want to hurt anything. I've seen you escort bugs out of the house. You don't swat flies. You catch them and put them outdoors. This time, you couldn't do that. There was nothing else to do. I'm proud of you."

Will was a little comforted. "So anyway, I think I'll leave the gun over at Morris' place for a couple months at least. Maybe someday I'll be able to think of targets and not see lives ending."

Harriet kissed him. "Meanwhile, your boys need you around, not playing this movie in your head."

"And they shall have me. Let's think of something happy. When and where would you like to get married?"

Harriet thought about it for a minute. "Bob's church, Maybe a year from now. No rush."

"Oh wow, he'd love that. I'll call him and find out what can happen." He went to the study. "Hi, Bob, Will MacLeish here, Could you marry us in your church?... Harriet and me, of course... right... I'm up here at my place in the country, with Harriet and her sons... Could you do it? I can imagine all kinds of restrictions... right... sure, when you can. Thanks, Bob, and thank you for introducing us. Might be the best thing to happen in my life. Talk to you later."

Back in the living room, Will advised Harriet. "He says he'd love to. He'll check if we can use the church, since I'm not a member."

Harriet found that frustrating. "Sheesh. Membership requirements. Meeting Bob, you'd think anyone was welcome for any reason."

"Yeah, but that's just Bob. The building belongs to the organization he works for. He said he would call the bishop."

"Okay, I guess. We can hope that the rules let Bob do what he wants. He's a great guy."

"I hope so. He's going to marry my daughter. I wonder if I should have the talk with him, tell him not to mess up."

Harriet giggled. "He's a priest, for goodness' sake. Not likely to even be rude to her."

"Point taken. Maybe we could have a backup plan. Like a picnic in Central Park with a dozen people and anybody who can doing the ceremony."

"A dozen people? I can imagine three dozen who would want to be at my wedding, minimum."

"Okay, so forty eight, at most. It could still pass as a picnic, and we wouldn't have to reserve space. I'm thinking that for functions, you have to let the park know what you're doing and where, and get a permit."

"Bob would know, from having arranged the festival when we met."

"Sure. When he calls back I'll ask." Something about the light streaming through the front window reminded Will of the first time he saw her standing by a window and he smiled.

"And what are you grinning at like a 4-year old on his first trip to a candy store?"

"You. I'm thinking of you standing next to the window. How much I felt, still feel every time I see you. How happy I am to have you in my life."

Harriet crossed to him. "And I still get amazed that you didn't run away, like a few other guys. That you included my sons as if you had known them all their lives. That you gave us the use of your house... that was too much to ask. It's a list of impossible things. Or at least I thought them impossible before I met you. Then I realize that I wanted to be with you long-term as soon as we met. My better angels told me so." A healthy dose of kissing ensued, followed by Maria's reaction of "Don't you two have your own room for that?"

Three hours later, the phone rang. Since he was sitting right next to it, Will answered. "Hi, Bob... yeah? That's great!... that's all?... right... right... sure. I'll let you know... thanks so much, I'll be in touch."

"Bob says he can marry us, in the church. He needs a two-week notice. We can just pick a date. And I looked it up: we go to the town clerk and apply for a marriage license, wait 24 hours and go for it. Is that too fast?"

Harriet shook her head. "Not really. The faster we can settle in to our new roles and put all our attention on living our lives, the better." More demonstrations of affection. This time, Maria just smiled.

....

A year later, Jorge and Manuel went "Out... just around." Promising to be back in a couple hours. Their first stop was Jane's house. "Miss Jane, could we talk to you about something?"

"Sure, guys... come on in. What's up?"

Manuel started. "Well, my mom and Mister Will, they're going to get married. We heard them talking about just going down to the courthouse, having hardly any ceremony."

Jorge continued. "And we think it would be better if there was more of a fuss. Like lots of people, their favorite pastor who introduced them, his parents and some friends. We know mom likes ceremonies... we've seen pictures from when she married our dad."

Jane thought for a minute. "Some friends from your old neighborhood?"

"Yeah. That would be great. Her friend James could probably round up some people. We have his phone number."

Jane grinned mischievously. "When are they thinking of doing this?"

"Next week, probably about noon on Friday. Mom can take the day off."

Jane wanted to hug the boys. "I think this is the best idea of the year. Let me make some calls and find out what we can arrange. This is just between us, right?"

Both boys nodded enthusiastically. When they left, Jane started calling. "Hi, Seamus?... our favorite writer thinks he can get married quietly, in a civil ceremony. I think it should be turned into a big freaking deal to surprise him... right... Harriet's sons brought up the idea... bring up some of their friends from the neighborhood... yeah, a guy named James, turns out he's a good friend... a bus? Sure, good idea... here's his number... they're thinking noon next Friday... right, not much time... I'm going to call Amy, and she'll call his parents... getting everybody there on time is the logistics nightmare... thanks, Seamus

One conspirator down, two to go. "Hi, Amy... I'm Will's
friend Jane... Will thinks he can get married quietly, not
much ceremony up here... right... anyway, Harriet's sons
even think it should be a big deal, with their favorite pastor,
a ceremony, and lots of friends... do you have his parents'
number?... great. You let them know.... I'll coordinate things
here, try to get a venue, some food... let me know how many
people you come up with... right... Thanks, hon... bye!"

Seamus made the first call. "Hi, Mister Weiss please...
hi, this is Seamus, Will MacLeish's agent... yes sir, not a bet
since... I'm calling to let you know that Will is getting
married... yeah. He thought he could have a quiet, tiny civil
ceremony, but the lady's two sons think it should be a big
deal... right... if you have any ideas, or if you'd like to come, a
friend of his from upstate is coordinating... we're thinking a
party would be nice... next Friday, about noon... here's her
number... Thanks, Mister Weiss, I know he'd love to see you
again... right... Bye, sir."

Amy made an immediate call too. "Hi, mom... Will is
getting married. He's trying for a quiet civil ceremony next
Friday about noon, but Harriet's sons think it should be a big
deal... right... do you have his parents' number?... yes
please... I'll pick a couple people in town and let them know...
it might be a good idea, if we wind up with a lot of folks, to
rent a bus... right... too bad it's not at night, we could do
fireworks... talk to you later, bye." Amy giggled at the thought
of turning her father's wedding into a national-holiday-grade
big deal."

Meanwhile, Jane had another call to make. "Hi, is this
James? Friend of Harriet Meron?... I'm a friend of Will
MacLeish, and Manuel and Jorge were just here. These two
are going to get married, and they're thinking of a small civil
ceremony about noon next Friday... the boys thought it
should be a bigger deal than that... right... so if a bunch of
people from the neighborhood could come up... we can
probably get a bus, so everybody doesn't have to drive...
right... by the way, do you know what her favorite music is? I
thought for the processional... oh that's wonderful...
thanks... I'm coordinating, so let me know... yeah, great fun.
Bye, nice talking to you."

Satisfied for the moment, Jane sat back with a glass of wine and watched "The Price is Right" for a while.

....

At 6:30, Jane's phone rang, and it kept ringing until 10:00. By the time she went to sleep, August 20th had nearly come together. A couple calls tomorrow and everything would be set. She could hardly sleep. She sent a text to Manuel "95% complete". She figured they would stop by in the morning. Hahaha, Will... you think you can sneak by without a big ceremony? Not quite. This village loves a wedding.

Throughout the ten days before Will and Harriet's big surprise, last-minute details came together. Harriet's wedding dress was chosen without her, and her favorite musician was magically drafted by a mutual friend. Will's parents and about two dozen neighbors were coming, with Lane; they would pick up Amy and Bob on the way.

Two busses had been secured at cost for neighbors and close friends from the neighborhood, and a map to their destination sent to James. Even at cost, the busses would cost $10,000. Fortunately, Jane had a plan. It would take another phone call.

"Hi, Will. I need a favor... $10,000, without explanation... right... if it's too much... oh Jesus you're good to us... I really appreciate this.... Thanks. See you in a little while."

Wait 'til he finds out what he paid for. He'd probably have been willing to spend twice that.

....

On the happy day, Maria took her grandsons out at 10:00 to "pick up a few things for a celebratory lunch for the family" after the wedding. Jane was making applesauce out of four bushels of freshly-picked apples in the morning, but promised that she and Morris wouldn't miss it for the world.

When Will and Harriet pulled up to the town offices, there was a sign on the door. "All city offices closed at this time. For services, come to the High School stadium." Will went back to the car to report this to Harriet. As they were thinking to come back Monday, Maria and the boys arrived.

The boys decided that today was a lucky day, and the group should at least follow the instructions to see what was happening. When they got to the High School parking lot, Will was surprised to see four busses in the parking lot. He asked the boys "Is there a big game today?"

"Oh, it's big alright." Manuel kept a straight face, but Jorge giggled. Leading them to the locker rooms, they sent Harriet into the girls' room. "Trust us. It's a surprise." Will got the same treatment.

Coming out onto the field, Harriet was already crying. A dressmaker from her building back in town had made an embroidered dress for her. "Now you look like a bride!" A hairdresser had come as well, and wove ribbons into her hair.

When Harriet saw the number of people standing on the field, and heard the first notes of "Samba pa Ti" being played, she staggered for a moment. Through her tears as her mother walked her toward where Bob and Will were standing. It was almost too much. Now she understood why the bride always walked slowly toward the altar. It took a lot of concentration not to fall on the ground crying.

Will just stood there in the tux Jane had rented for him, beaming. The most beautiful human being in his world had been transformed into the princess she deserved to be seen as.

When Harriet took her place in front of Bob, the music became quieter, but continued. She noticed two people standing behind him. Bob started talking. "Ladies and gentlemen, we are here to witness the wedding of Harriet and William, which I hope to claim some credit for. You see, I had the pleasure of introducing them.

"I won't make a big speech, despite having one all written. I think I know a prayer that will say everything that needs to be said.

"Our father, who art in heaven..." the crowd joined in "Hallowed be thy name. Thy kingdom come, thy will be done on earth as it is in Heaven. Give us this day our daily bread, and forgive us as we forgive those who trespass against us, and lead us not into temptation but deliver us from evil, Amen." The crowd fell silent.

"Ladies and gentlemen, our guest celebrants: the Episcopal Archbishop of New York Samuel Craig, and my own Bishop Simm."

The two men spoke together. "Lord bless this couple, that they may always happily express your love for the world and their love for one another."

Bob spoke again. "Please rise... If anyone have any objection to this marriage speak now or forever hold your peace." As he paused, laughter erupted in the crowd. "There being no objection, we will proceed. Harriet, do you take William..." she had stopped shaking when she looked into Will's eyes "Yes".

"To be your lawful husband... yes... to have and to hold... yes... from this day forward... yes... 'til death do you part?"

"Yes yes yes!" Harriet wrapped her arms around Will's neck and kissed him.

Trying hard not to rush things, Bob continued. He knew he didn't have to ask the question, that everyone in attendance could answer it. "William, do you take Harriet...I do... for your lawful wife... (too busy kissing)... to have and to hold from this day forward 'til death do you part?"

It took Will a moment to free his voice. "I do."

Bob had just the one more happy thing to say. "By the power vested in me, in the presence of this company and undoubtedly the presence of God, I hereby pronounce you husband and wife. You can stop kissing one another any time now."

The crowd erupted in laughter and cheers and swept forward to congratulate the new couple. Giving it a couple of minutes, Bob stepped to the microphone again. "Ladies and gentlemen, if you please return to your seats for another few minutes, there is another piece of business here.

"As some of you know, I recently became engaged to marry a wonderful woman, Amy Leary. The recommended one-year waiting period between proposal and ceremony having elapsed, I would like to marry her now.

"So Amy, if you would join me here, the Bishop has consented to marry us."

Amy screamed, paused, and when Bob held out his hand ran to him. Bob stepped around the microphone and the Bishop took over. "Friends, relatives and loved ones, I have the privilege of marrying Robert and Amy. I have known Robert since he entered the seminary, and I have spoken with Amy enough to know that these two belong together.

"Folks, this might be the fastest religious ceremony ever performed, so don't blink. Robert and Amy: knowing as you do the responsibilities of a husband and wife within the Church, do you accept one another as partners in everything, for life, whatever life has to offer?"

Bob yelled "YES!"

The Bishop looked at Amy, who wiped her hand down her face to relax her smile enough to speak, and said as loudly "YES".

The bishop massaged his ear, and continued. "Having accepted one another, and by the acceptance of these rings provided by your parishioners, I now declare you husband and wife. You should kiss one another now."

And yes, they kissed. They got lost in the kiss. They didn't even hear the roar and cheering that rose from the crowd.

When the happy noise subsided a bit, Michael Weiss stepped up to the microphone. "Ladies and gentlemen, there is a feast waiting to be had in the cafeteria. This way, everyone." He shepherded everyone in the right direction.

The cafeteria smelled familiar to Will, the scent of Michael's restaurant. Once everyone was seated with a plate of food and another of salad, Michael proposed a toast. "To the brides and grooms: Long life, great health, overwhelming joy, and almost more love than you can bear. Salud!" The crowd agreed.

In a quiet moment, Will found Bob by himself. "So when did you kids get the License?"

"Oh, that... we haven't. Technically, the Church doesn't require a Civil license to marry people. We can get the legal stuff taken care of in the coming week, and have another wedding, the civil one."

Satisfied that his friend hadn't pulled a fast one, Will dragged him over to the Bishop and Archbishop, now in street clothes, who were having a discussion of morality. Will wanted to get in on this.

....

The buses back to Harriet's old neighborhood left at 6:00, and the bus back toward Will's parents' house took off shortly after. Michael's staff had the cafeteria back to its original state by 6:30, and having helped with cleanup Bob's congregation dragged Bob and Amy into a bus at 6:35. With appropriate hugs from Will and Harriet, they were off. The last people to leave were the newly expanded MacLeish clan, Michael and his staff.

Will commented "This was fantastic. Thanks for catering, Mister Weiss."

Michael admitted "It's not all me. Seamus picked up half, the lawyers pitched in, Bob's congregation, and Harriet's former neighbors too. This whole thing only cost me about $3.00 a plate. To be able to brag that I catered Will MacLeish's wedding, that's cheap. Thought maybe we could take a picture I could hang on the wall."

"Sure." The photographer had come with the restaurant crew. One shot and it was done.

Michael had the next question. "Do you know who that guitarist was? She's fantastic."

Harriet knew. "She's one of my neighbors back in town. She's 16, and records tracks for the neighborhood recording studio. Her name is Maqaia. James asked her to come, and she said yes if she could bring her mom. Neither of them get out of the city much."

Michael nodded. "That explains them sitting outside with some folks for a couple hours. Breathing some fresh air."

Harriet turned to Will. "A few people said they'd like to live someplace like this. We might get an influx."

Will decided that would be good. "More people paying taxes means the rate won't go up as fast, and more people working gets us more goods and services. No down side." Harriet nodded.

Manuel and Jorge had an announcement. "We think we'd like to use MacLeish for our last name. Make this a whole new life." Harriet and Will hugged them.

About this time, Michael apologetically turned to go. "Have to get the crew into their beds. We can be closed for Friday, but not Saturday. They've got a 14 hour day to rest up for. Drop by sometime… dinner's on me."

As the crew boarded their own bus and pulled out, the High School Principal emerged. "That's about the happiest thing that's happened here since our first graduation. Thanks for having it here."

Will didn't want the credit to get misdirected. "Jane did it. Jane Taylor made all those arrangements."

The boys fell asleep as soon as they got home. Four hours of dancing and flirting plus two good meals each added up to unconsciousness. Harriet guessed that they would wake up in about twelve hours. She and Will stayed up until midnight, listening to some music then sitting on the porch wondering what the future would be.

And so we leave our pair of loving pairs

Sitting happily on their own front stairs

Gazing far into midnight's darkened sphere

To see what in happy futures might appear.

We wish them all the good their lives can fit

And all the grace enough to deal with it.